ROGUES
OF THE
CROSSLANDS

Azorias'
Blade

ROGUES
OF THE
CROSSLANDS

Azorias' Blade

JOHN DAZE

This book is dedicated to my loving wife and children for tolerating my newfound passion. Of course, Mom, and Bill, Alex, Delores & Senior. To my old tabletop gaming family—Damon, Nykone, and Angie—thank you for your inspiration, dedication, and traveling so far to play on the weekends. To Jimmy, John H., and that fateful impromptu game with my CP crew. To Dwarven Forge, and to Nick and his team at Dynamic Forces. Lastly, to Trevor, Terica, Michael, Joe, and Jody—thank you for your inspiration and mentorship.

ADVISORY

This book contains material that may not be suitable for all readers. There are subjects related to racism amongst mythical races, violence involving elven children, addiction, disease and death.

FOREWORD

Long ago, when the earth was new, it bore mythical creatures only spoken of in today's legends. They lived together in blissful harmony. It was a time when elves and giants built magnificent dwellings while sprites and gnomes tended to the bountiful lands that fed and healed them. The beings of young earth had never known of evil until Zelphar, a Celestial of great renown, descended from the heavens, took shape, and hid among the elves of Galvardia.

Galvardia's bravest and most beautiful elf warrior was D'Asora. She was the adventurous kind and took a liking to the mysterious newcomer. Soon, the liking blossomed into true love. Before long, they were married and conceived a baby girl.

Unbeknownst to the people of Galvardia, Zelphar closely guarded a secret only shared with D'Asora. He came to earth as a refugee, escaping a great demon invasion. The demons, called Asharyins by the elves, eventually hunted Zelphar down and killed him. Devastated by her true love's death, D'Asora collected *his blood and brought it to the last remaining protector of Galvardia, the great Klarion Dragon. The dragon sacrificed his life by giving her the strongest known material, which were the scales that protected his heart. The magical scales, imbued with Zephar's blood and a single tear from D'Asora's, created the mythical Klarion Blade. She dedicated the remaining years of her life to hunting down the Asharyin demons with the sword. Her bloodline continues to honor the oath, hoping to finally rid the earth of the demons.*

CHAPTER

One

A GIRL AND HER BLADE

The reflection of the violent fire danced in her yellow eyes. The heat from the flames just about seared her skin. Little Azoria stood motionless, surrounded by the inferno. The sword's blade in her right hand erupted in bright sparks of neon blue. Her mouth was open in a gasp, exposing her fear and confusion. Her eyes fixed on the giant green creatures slashing down everyone in sight. Friends, neighbors, elders; all were dead or dying by then. The horde had struck with such fury that the little elven girl couldn't fathom the destruction encircling her. *Run*, Azoria told herself. To her right, freedom with her friends. To her left was a chance to find her father. The future of the Crosslands depended on her decision.

The Evening Before

AVERSTONE WAS A QUIET LITTLE VILLAGE DEEP IN THE HEART OF THE wildwood forest. Finding it was challenging, and only a few dirt roads led there. That time of year, rooftops were gifted with hyper-real colors of pink and purple cherry blossom petals. The village nestled between the creek to the east and the hills with the green crystals to the west. Thickets and untold beasts surrounded them.

There was one intrepid elfin girl in Averstone by the name of Azoria Dash. She was the most daring of her friends and yearned for adventure. It was the season of the storms, and that evening, the thunder brought a sleeping Azoria to painful lucidity. Her mother, Janella, had died birthing her just twelve years before. Even though she did not recall what her mother looked like, Azoria swore her mother came and spoke to her. Her mom's voice left a sleeping Azoria with warm tears running from her closed eyes. She talked to Azoria in an unfamiliar language that shook her awake.

Careful not to disturb her father's slumber, Azoria quietly made her way to the wooden chest that held her late mother's belongings. She wrapped herself in her mom's clothes and rummaged through various trinkets. Along with a few pieces of jewelry, Azoria discovered a short sword, unlike anything she had seen before. The shiny handle matched the luster of its sheath with intricate embellishments and designs. Depictions ran across the metallic portions like a flowing mural. She lightly ran her tiny fingertips over the grooves of the smooth etchings. The sword was so light that it felt like nothing was in her hands. The cross-guard at the top of the handle looked as if it was wrapped with rose stems and dipped in silver. A single thorn spike protruded from the rose stems, also forged in silver.

Azoria gazed in awe at its radiance as she withdrew it from the metallic-looking sheath. The blade was translucent, like glass. Cutting herself on the thorny spike, she instantly dropped the sword.

For a glass-looking blade, the sword was quite durable. It bounced against the blade's edge and landed without damage. She carefully picked it up again, cautiously searching for any more spikes. As Azoria examined it closer, she noticed the blade itself radiated a tinge of blue light.

The sudden sound of heavy footsteps shook the old wooden floor. Behind her stood her father, Gradian. "Azoria, it's late. What are you doing up?"

He found her in one of her mother's gowns that was far too long. "I couldn't sleep. Something called out to me in my dreams. I don't know, but it may have been Mom."

Gradian smiled, "I remember when I taught you to count the constellation's stars to fall asleep."

"Fifty-seven, Dad. Still fifty-seven stars."

Gradian moaned as he took a seat on the floor next to Azoria, reminding her of his aging body. He was bigger than most elves and his size gave him the advantage when he was a younger warrior, but his old injuries now diminished his movements. He walked with a cane due to a constant limp and his back would give out, leaving him in bed for days at a time. The thick scars worn across his arms and chest told a story of survival in wars past. He fought on the side of humans and later fought against them during the Great Disorder. The scars were more than physical, however. They, along with the birth of his daughter, eventually changed him to search for peace through the works of his crafting shop.

Growing old confused young Azoria. While the gray hairs speckled her father's face like spilt salt, she could never imagine him so broken. She refused to believe it, and so did the others in Averstone. Behind the calm voice and friendly demeanor burrowed a scrappy fighter. His tired eyes told the story of a man who loved and lost. Gradian missed his wife, but he sought refuge from the pain through the love of his only daughter.

"Oh, how I miss her." He looked at Azoria and grinned. "You have her smile. Unfortunately, you have her stubbornness too."

They both looked at the mess of clothes tossed about. She felt shameful for going through the chest, "I'm sorry I woke you. I know you told me not to rummage through her things, but I couldn't get this voice out of my head. It was like something was telling me to find the sword."

"I'm not mad. In fact, I figured this day would come." Gradian replied. "There's a lot to tell you, but I was waiting until you were older. I believe that some things can wait."

Gradian tried his best to hide that world from Azoria, but eventually, her calling would come. Like the matriarchs before her, the calling arrived on their sixteenth birthday. It was uncommon for the sword to call out at such a young age. Gradian believed she, indeed, wasn't ready.

"Look out the window," Gradian told her. "Each constellation you see is a god who shepherds the stars and planets around them. There are many gods spread across the universe. As you know, our god is Tira'Sora. She brings light to our darkness."

Azoria had all these stories memorized and sarcastically mimicked his words as he spoke them. "I know. I've heard the legends before."

"Okay, Zorie. Do you see that bright red light spinning to the east?

Azoria had seen it before, especially on clear nights. Sometimes, she and her friends would sit at the village center and hear the elders tell them stories of the menacing titan. She looked in the direction where her father pointed. There it was, hovering over the earth like a hurricane just beyond the stars—The Drojokan. Its ominous red and black flares violently spiraled in the night sky, siphoning all the light around it into its' voracious belly. The constellation's stars tearing apart, one by one, desperately clawing to escape. For many, their struggles were futile as they were pulled into the gigantic cloud's gravity. Those lucky enough to break free its grasp tumbled to the earth as falling stars. Drojokan's hunger remained incessantly growing over the centuries. It meticulously searched for any constellation to feed upon. Tira'Sora stood in the beasts' path.

"That's Drojakon." Azoria asserted.

"That's right. The elders say it's the dark realm. It's in constant battle against the constellations. Drojakon is forever pulling them closer. In the same manner that death pulls us near. It's said that one day, Drojakon will pull in and devour all the light around it. Even us. It feeds from the light and lives in the darkness."

Azoria's eyes drew over the countless shining orbs across the black sky. "Oh, did you see that falling star?" She questioned in awe.

"Those are Tira'Sora's Celestials." Gradian continued. "They're the heavenly warriors whom the Drojakon defeated. They scatter amongst her planets to outrun Drojakon's wrath. However, Drojakon sends its' Asharyins to hunt down the Celestials on earth and devour them. In our world, the Asharyins wait amongst the shadows. These demons whisper to the earthly beings and persuade them to commit evils against each other. As mortals, we are all easily persuaded by the Asharyins to commit sins against each other. They use us to lure the Celestials out, who hide among this earth. That's what ignited the Great Disorder."

"So, since we'll all be pulled into the Drojakon anyways, what's the point in fighting it?"

"Because light is hope." Gradian smiled. "If even the tiniest glimmer of light exists, then so does hope."

Gradian's words inspired Azoria to ask more questions about the legends.

"Azoria, do not concern yourself with these things now. There'll be time. You have one moment in life to be a child, and this is yours. Enjoy your youth."

They sat together as he told her of times past, enjoying the lighthearted evening that strengthened their bond as father and daughter. It had been a while since they'd spent precious time together. She had so many questions about the sword, but that night was too perfect to spoil. Like always, the stories eventually drifted into typical lessons of life and philosophy. He appreciated her innocence and wanted to keep it that way for as long as possible.

"I love you, Zorie. Always remember, love is stronger than a sword. But be careful, for so is hate."

There was more to tell Azoria, but Gradian believed it was not time. Instead, he kissed her on her forehead and returned to his room. She'd promised him she would return everything back to the chest, but Azoria had other intentions. She couldn't control her urge to show the sword off to her friends in the morning.

Every dawn, the elfin children of Averstone met near the creek to fetch water for the villagers. Like most children, the elfins spent more time playing at the creek than doing their chores. "Never go past the creek," the elders would lecture the elfins. Unpleasant surprises occupied the forest, and the elders discouraged exploring the world outside. The worry was not in vain; some little ones had dared to go alone and never returned.

The elfins at the creek included her two best friends, Gymmal and Myra. Gymmal was a few years older than Azoria and was deemed an honorary big brother to many. Always the adventurous type, he loved to show off his athleticism. Gymmal enjoyed the reaction of his younger audience. One thing he was always with was his boomerang. Gymmal was so quick that he could throw it in one direction and race past it to catch it before it returned. He performed these kinds of tricks for the elders during village festivities.

Myra, on the other hand, was shy. Her demeanor was always calm and subtle. Often creating music and poetry, Myra enjoyed sharing her artistry with her closest friends. Myra's singing voice was beautiful and soothing, much like the trance-inducing sounds of sirens. Even with her talents, she was soft-spoken. There was an air of innocence about Myra that encouraged her to see the good in everyone. Her maturity aged well beyond her youth. If Gymmal was considered the big brother, Myra was the mother figure.

Azoria was quite the opposite of her friends. A tad shorter than Myra and Gymmal, she made up for it with bravery. Azoria was resilient. Her confidence was often mistaken for disrespect. Her father had difficulty controlling her cheekiness. She was known for challenging the teens in their warrior activities, like wrestling and hunting. Even though she lost to them, she always swore to come back stronger. Myra would calmly reassure her to never give up.

"I've had dreams of you doing great things, Azoria. There will be a day when those who doubt you will be the ones who follow you," Myra said. Azoria would shake off her disappointment and return a quirky smile.

The elfins were quite impressed when Azoria arrived at the creek with the sword that morning.

"That's quite a special-looking...toy. Where'd you get it?" Gymmal asked as he studied Azoria's new find.

"I don't think it's a toy. I found it in my mom's old stuff." Azoria's eyes were engaged on the blade as Gymmal passed it to Myra.

"It's beautiful," Myra said, carefully inspecting the handle's designs. "There's some writing on the blade. I can't make it out."

Azoria squinted her eyes. "Yeah, me neither. Doesn't look elven. Maybe it's common speak?"

"I don't think so. My father taught me some common speak, which doesn't look like it," Gymmal said.

"Let's test it out," Azoria suggested.

"If it's glass, it might break. May not be a good idea," countered Gymmal.

"I don't think they'd make a sword that could damage so easily." Azoria laughed.

In excitement, Azoria ran over to the first thing she saw that she believed would challenge the blade's sharpness. Ankle deep in the water, she clopped to a large rock that split the creek into two smaller streams. The dark gray rock was roughly twice her height.

Years of weather had naturally shaped the rock to give it smooth sides and sharp edges, like a giant arrowhead. She gripped the sword with two hands and swung at it. To her surprise, a bright blue spark cleanly blasted pieces of the rock that the blade made contact with. Gray fragments splintered off and sprayed about them.

Many elfins nearby covered their faces to protect themselves from the flying debris. Then they crowded around Azoria in amazement. Some clapped, while others drew blank stares. They hadn't seen anything like it before. Azoria brought the sword back to her side. Her mouth dropped in sheer marvel. She had so many questions, but the blade would surely not answer just yet.

"Oh, no, Zorie. Look," the youngest of the elfins, Sariah called to Azoria in alarm. Myra's little sister, Sariah, possessed the same calmness and empathy as her older sibling. They all turned as Sariah looked down at the fluttering osprey chick knocked from its nest. A small shard was stuck in its side, piercing its thin wing. "I think it's hurt."

"Sariah, do that thing you do to help fix animals," one elfin said. Sariah possessed an exceptional talent that was unique to her family. Being so young, she could only perform her ability on small creatures and when the sun was out.

She sat on the wet grass near the creek shore, cupped her hand, and scooped the chick up. She raised the other hand to the sky, palm up.

"Watch this. It's one of the best things I've ever seen!" Gymmal nudged Azoria.

"I know. I've seen it before, too. It's always great!"

Sariah's palms turned bright orange. Like a conduit, the sunlight transferred from her raised arm, through her body and out of her other hand. The chick, chirping in fear, began flapping its injured wing. The rock fell onto the ground as the wound healed shut.

She placed the chick on the ground as the mother osprey hovering overhead picked it up and returned to its nest.

With the elfins so focused on Sariah, they missed the young Averstone warriors returning from the dark woodlands beyond the creek. It was a hunting party, with two carrying a deer on a wooden pole. The rest of the warriors were ahead, chopping through the brush and creating a makeshift trail with machetes. After a kill, it was tradition to take its blood and draw three lines down their faces with their fingertips. Each line was a sign of respect for the prey, the hunter, and the earth.

Because of their youth, the elders assigned the young warriors the most arduous duties in Averstone. Known as the Stone Harpies, they were named after the mighty harpy eagles that lived in the trees above their village. The cost of the harpies' hard work was their blind arrogance. One of many traditions among the wildwood elves was the harsh treatment they inflicted on the elfins. Next in line to become future warriors, they were to learn how to defend themselves against the harpies picking on them. And rightfully so. Elfins were expected to become the future defenders of their homeland.

"Look at what the kiddies have." Ollie and his crew leaped over a few boulders, splashing through the ice-cold water.

"Give it up, Ollie. Don't you get tired of being an oaf?" Gymmal said, interrupting their laughing, his useless attempt to show courage.

"Shut up, Gymmal. If I wasn't friends with your brother, I'd smash you on the rocks," Ollie threatened, shoving his fist near Gymmal's face.

"Whatchu got there, anyways? A new toy for the babies?" another sarcastic harpy yelled out.

Azoria attempted to hide it by quickly sliding it back into the sheath over her shoulder. The harpies were known for taking things from the elfins and not returning them. She hoped that with all the attention on Gymmal, they'd pay no mind to the sword. That didn't happen.

"Hey, Zorie, not so fast. Lemme see it," Ollie said.

"I can't. It belongs to my mom... Well, it used to, anyway."

Ollie moved closer to Azoria. "Since your mom's dead, I don't think she'd mind if I took a quick look."

Azoria fumed with anger. She shot a look of detest at the harpy leader. "Well, my dad's still alive, and I don't think he'd like it very much."

That was true. Gradian was well respected in the village. Usually, the harpies would have backed off after hearing his name. Under normal circumstances, they'd be more respectful to his only daughter to avoid his wrath. But the harpies were brimming with adrenaline from their kill.

Azoria had no intention of giving up the sword. When she turned to face Ollie, however, she felt the sword removed from her back. Before she knew it, one of the harpies behind her had it in his hand.

"This is nice, Zorie. Definitely made for a girl." The harpy cracked.

"Let me see it." Ollie reached out his hand. Before he could grab it, a boomerang whizzed past his head. It was so close he felt the wind swat across his cheek.

"Next time, I won't miss," Gymmal warned, catching the returning boomerang.

"Little guy has some courage, huh?" Another teen laughed. "I think you're being disrespectful to Ollie. Apologize."

"No, it's okay." Ollie grabbed the sword anyway, daring Gymmal. Then he ignorantly examined it. "Let's give them their toy back. Zorie, go ahead and take it. Here you go."

As Azoria extended her hand, Ollie turned and threw the sword as far out into the woods as he could. It landed somewhere past the creek and into the thick of the forest. "Fetch, babies!"

Azoria's heart sank. The most precious of her mom's possessions may be lost for good. Her father was surely going to be angry. She second-guessed her decision to bring the sword out. The elfins stood there, equally disheartened. When they thought the teens couldn't be any ruder, the harpies discovered a new low.

"Harpies, let's move out," Ollie commanded.

He gave Gymmal a dirty look to intimidate him. Gymmal raised his boomerang, imagining himself throwing it at the back of Ollie's head as the warriors continued to the village.

Myra, always the voice of reason, assured Gymmal. "Ollie's trouble. Everyone knows it. One day, he'll get his. I'm sure of it."

"Don't worry about it," six-year-old Sariah roared. "He's like a tree—all bark!" Her voice was too cute to be taken seriously.

The elfins laughed, breaking the tension.

"Uhhh, I don't think that's how it goes," Myra said.

"Sure it is!" Sariah retorted, giving her a smug look.

As everyone laughed at the conversation, Gymmal remained quiet. He was obviously disappointed in himself. Gymmal was strong for his age, but the elfins knew he wasn't much of a match for the stronger harpies. He kicked a rock and began making his way to the creek water.

Azoria saw where he was headed. "No, it's fine. I'll go get the sword." She jumped into the creek past Gymmal and towards the dark woods.

"Zorie, we're not supposed to be out there," Gymmal said.

To compound the problem, her search would be more difficult due to the sword's clear blade. Azoria was losing both hope and patience. "I'm so dumb for bringing it out here. My dad's going to kill me!"

"Are you sure you don't want me to go?" asked Gymmal.

"No. I said I'll go." Without hesitation, Azoria hiked through the brush, pushing the tall grass out of the way. Everything was still wet from the rains the night before, soaking her pants and shirt.

Dew glistened from the shiny dogwood leaves to the giant webs of the orb weaver spiders. Before her stood a wall of greenery several stories high. Azoria finally found a dark void stretched out just wide enough for her to fit through. Vines and tree roots intermingled on the thick, grassy forest floor. Tree branches connected overhead like giant handshakes. Ferns and ivory reached up and coiled over the dense trees, competing for the sunlight breaking through the leafy canopies. While all was still, an intense feeling of a thousand eyes were watching her every step. The mist below her knees made it difficult to see her feet. The condensation soaked into her boots.

She entered the forest like an unwelcome visitor. Ahead, the endless vines entangled her like tentacles, interrupting her every step.

She pulled apart the overgrowth around her to clear a path, to no avail. Nature was stronger than her little arms. Several times, she slipped and fell into a mosaic of shrubbery. One hanging branch snapped back as she pushed it away, leaving a small slice on her cheek. It was as if the woods defiantly refused her presence. It defended itself with each attempt. Both opponents stubbornly refused to concede. Under the bravado lay fear. Azoria couldn't shake the elders' disturbing legends about the dark woods beyond the creek. The deeper into the forest she went, the darker it got.

"You see it?" Gymmal called out, no longer able to see her.

"Not yet." Azoria took a few more steps into the foreign land. She suddenly realized that was the farthest she had ever gone. It was scary. Her skin shivered from the fear. Yet oddly enough, the fear was invigorating. Azoria may have traveled a mere few yards away, but the crowded foliage made her feel she was far from her friends.

The temperature seemed to lower by twenty degrees. Azoria felt alone and vulnerable on this side of the creek. She could have been a million miles from Averstone and not know the difference. Looking through those woods was like peering into a black window with no reflection. Cold and wet; the two things she hated. She scrambled about, searching high and low for her sword. "*Acha!*" Azoria cursed in her native tongue as she peered into the endless green. "How far did he throw it?"

She heard it before she saw it. There was a light whisper in her ear, the same comforting voice she heard the night before that woke her up. The voice guided her closer to the sword, encouraging her in a language she had never heard. Confidence returned in her chest as she breathed in, realizing that she wasn't alone. Finally, there it was. The blade laid on its side, buzzing with a light blue tint, and its shiny, stainless handle reflecting what little sunlight touched it.

She crouched to retrieve it and noticed sudden movement on her left. It wasn't Gymmal nor Myra. The harpies had undoubtedly made it back to the village by then. Whatever she was seeing, it was too large and noisy to be elf-kind. Even though it was rather far away, Azoria made out the muscular shape of the figure with green skin. As it moved closer, its skin tone reminded her of the murky foam that sometimes builds around stagnant crevices of the creek's runoffs. Its body was covered in tattoos. Its hair was sculpted into a mohawk, with the shaved sides exposing more tattoos. The back of the mohawk ran down into large, chunky braids. The thing had short fangs that protroded from its bottom lip. An iron ring hung from its nose which vaguely resembling a pig snout. She had never seen anything like it. It wasn't the thing that scared her, but what it represented. There was something ominous about how it moved, heading closer to the village.

What is that? Azoria asked herself. The thing was tall, nearly seven feet. She remained crouched, carefully watching the figure. Several others appeared behind him. None were empty-handed. Some held large weapons, while others grasped thick roped nets.

Something's wrong, she thought. The wildwood elves learned to move about without a sound at a young age. Elves were notably quicker than most other races, even though she had no way of knowing. The sword protested her silence, with the blade transitioning from a dim blue into a bright burst of glowing neon. The shine illuminated the little space she found herself in. It gave off a vibration that shifted to a high-pitched sound, like the tines of a tuning fork. Keeping an eye on the beasts, she hurried to sheath the dancing sword. Quickly, Azoria darted back to the creek. It seemed as if every inch of vegetation purposely made it more arduous than the last. Panic washed over her as she pressed between the foliage. Finally throwing caution away, she forcefully broke through branches and vines, causing birds to shoot out of bushes, and leaves sputtering behind her. Every crack and snap meant progress. But for each step she took, the monsters took a dozen. Her heart pounded wildly at the thought of the beasts advancing closer to Averstone while she remained hemmed in nature's trap. Azoria's efforts didn't go unpunished. When she finally made it out to her friends, cuts and scratches draped across her small frame.

"You found your sword! We were about to come look for you," Myra said.

"Shhh! There's something out there. Big green people with pig faces!"

Gymmal responded with bewilderment. "Orcs?"

"I don't know!" Azoria attempted to piece together how the elders described them in stories.

One of the elfins looked up at the sky and sharply twitched her nose. The others started breathing deeply.

"Does anybody smell smoke?" Sariah asked.

Usually, that time of year brought the sweet scents of the bright cherry blossoms. Spring was the most crucial season in the wildwoods, resembling rebirth. The elfins would play in the piles of fallen pink and purple petals as they did with the winter snow. At that moment, however, something was off. There was electricity in the air, a feeling of danger they couldn't verbalize.

"No, I don't smell… Wait a minute." Gymmal sniffed at the air, trying to reassure himself. They stood quietly, looking at each other for confirmation. Then there was a break in the silence.

It happened so fast. Screams abruptly permeated the sky over Averstone. Gymmal looked back at Azoria. The younger elfins cried out in shock.

"What was that?" Myra asked.

It happened again.

"I'm scared," cried Sariah, shivering.

A third wave of screams shot out from the village. Without a thought, the kids rushed up the hill, their little hearts pounding out of their chests. Their tiny feet pushed upward in dismay. As the next one made it up, they helped the ones behind. They didn't know what to expect; whether to run toward the horrific sounds or run away. Something was clear, however. They wanted to be with their families. Whatever was happening, there was an innate awareness that home was safe. They were sure whatever it was, the brave moms, dads, big brothers and sisters, elders, and warriors would fight it off and win. This was Averstone, home of the most valiant wildwood elves in the land. That's what they told themselves.

Over the hill, they charged back onto the deer trail and sprinted back. The elfins could see massive plumes of smoke above the tree lines before they reached the little village. Walls of black and gray fumes confronted them, throwing off their bearings. The sound of roaring fires whipped in the wind, and so did the cries of Averstone's residents. Between the patches of dense smoke, Azoria observed the familiar huts of her fellow elves engulfed in fire. What was once green and lush had become bright hues of blood orange. The fires pounced from torched arrows and slithered from structure to structure.

Those giant green men she'd seen earlier were now running through her village. The size of the orcs was disturbingly larger than the elves they'd blitzed. All of them were built like statues, with hair in different shapes and vibrant colors. They roared like lions as they smashed everything in their path. The small dirt roads were littered with the bodies of those who'd attempted to defy them. Each body was someone the elfins knew. They screamed and pointed at each one they encountered, calling out their names in horror. Every inch of Averstone was under destruction.

The children stopped in the center of town to take it all in. Chaos surrounded them. Lifeless and dying bodies sprawled across the earthen ground and blood-soaked cobblestones. Some were motionless, twisted in unnatural forms with arrows embedded in them; others were missing limbs. Azoria saw the children cry out in horror as Gymmal picked up Sariah to cover her eyes. Panic poured over them as they took in all they saw.

Is this real? Is this really happening? Azoria asked herself. *Please wake up, Zorie, please!* She slapped her face in desperation.

There were futile skirmishes everywhere, some brave elves with swords drawn clashing against the opposing and unstoppable forces before them.

JOHN DAZE

Azoria had never seen an orc in real life, but she'd heard of their savagery. She'd learned the tales of the old battles that her father would tell her on stormy nights. She'd heard all about the heroics of when the wildwood elves had battled side-by-side with the humans of Varos to defeat them.

Now, with the mayhem all-consuming, the orcs finished hacking through the last of the defenders and turned their attention to the screaming children.

Gymmal looked over at Azoria. "We're safer in the forest! Help me get the kids out of here!"

Azoria shook her head in defiance. "No, you take them! I need to find my father."

Gymmal reached out with his free hand to one of the other elf-ins. "If your father is alive, he wouldn't want you running around here! We need to go now!"

The little one who grabbed Gymmal's hand cried out. "Where's my mommy and daddy? Are they dead too?"

Azoria withdrew the blade. "I'm finding my dad! I know he's alive, and I bet he's already cut down a dozen of them!"

Gymmal gave her one last look, desperate for her to go with him.

"I love you, friends!" she yelled to them. "Go. Now!"

Without hesitation, Gymmal herded the children back out of Averstone. Azoria, seeing the orcs stomping in their direction, waved to bait them to her. "Hey, over here!"

As the orcs split up, a few of them directed their chase after Azoria. Having the advantage of knowing her way, she dashed off past a row of burning cottages to throw them off. It wasn't easy, as billows of wind-blown smoke drew her into confusion. The smoke lined the inside of her nostrils. She could taste it as it coated her teeth. She could feel it in her lungs as she ran. Eventually, she found her way home.

Her stinging, irritated eyes trailed the fire over her cottage. It angrily reached upward like a monstrous red and black snake striking the sky. The force from the heat was intense, keeping her at bay.

Waves of hot air slammed into her, sizzling her sweat. Next to the house were her father's bird cages. The doors were open, and all the birds were missing. They were the only things not on fire. She looked up and saw dozens of Gradian's prized golden wrens franticly flying to the east. Worry set in. Even though she stood merely feet away from all her burning belongings, her only thought was to find her father.

There he was, lying face down, trapped under the incinerated rubble that was once their home. She ran to her father and struggled to pull the debris off him. It was too heavy. After several attempts, she finally crouched next to him. Azoria delicately held his charred hand. The skin slid off through Azoria's fingers. She noticed his bracelet was missing. Every clan leader wore the bracelet of their family's emblem, gold and silver chains intertwined. It was gone. Her eyes welled with tears, making it hard to see. The weight of the debris pushed on his chest as he struggled to breathe. Her heart dropped as she witnessed her symbol of strength become so weak and helpless. The last bit of life in him squeezed her hand. Trembling, Azoria asked, "Can you hear me? Can you move? Please get up."

She heard him whisper a few broken phrases. "The sword? Do you have it?"

Realizing she was never supposed to take it, Azoria was flushed with fear. She knew her dad was disappointed when she decided not to listen to him, but now she felt immense remorse. Even at his weakest, he was intimidating.

"Dad, I'm so sorry. I took it to the creek to show my friends. I was going to bring it back."

"No, my dear, it's okay. You need to take it and…"

"And what, Daddy?" She hadn't called him that in years. She felt too old to speak to him like a child, but in a way, it comforted them both. She wanted to take him to a much better time.

"And what?"

His stony hand squeezed hers as he released his final breath. Just as quickly, his hand fell limp. As his soul exited his body, she felt comfort and security leave hers. *What happens now?* She was truly alone. The only person she ever relied on, the center of her universe, was gone. Her mind was nowhere and everywhere all at once. Her home was destroyed, her friends were gone, and her father had been killed. Azoria was truly alone.

There were too many questions and no time to internalize. As her father released his final breath, she heard galloping horse hooves charging nearby. While others may have hidden in the horror of the situation, she only felt one emotion—pure hatred. Azoria raised to confront the savage horde, but they raced away from Averstone. The orcs on horseback seemed more focused on other things than the small girl. She swung her sparkling blue sword in the air and screamed as they exited the town.

Her heart pumped anger through her veins. She saw the horses race into the Crosslands and head east. There was no way she could keep up. But that was something else she paid no attention to. Like a zombie, she simply began walking toward the east, entering the forest. She had no idea what awaited her or whether she'd even reach the orcs. Vengeance was sure to carry her farther than her feet could take her.

EMPTY BOTTLES LITTERED THE CABIN FLOOR. JANDAR HADN'T MOVED all day. One bootless leg hung off the bed as he snored heavily from his open mouth. His face was covered in gray and black stubble that resembled ash. His skin was cracked and sunburned. Even through his weathered exterior, Jandar hardly resembled any trace of elf attributes. A half-breed—though he looked more human—lacking the characteristic pointy ears.

Armed with his faithful bow, his reputation as one of the grandest shadow rangers in the Crosslands had quickly eroded. Jandar's recent venture earned him a decent living as a trekker. Travelers trusted him to guide them about the Crosslands safely. They paid handsomely for his expertise. He'd returned home a few nights before. It was considered a harrowing adventure to the average citizen, but to Jandar, it was just another assignment. The last job had taken him from the border of the Varosian empire in the east to escort settlers to a fort in the west. It was too dangerous for settlers to make it on their own. Jandar was very knowledgeable of the Crosslands' terrain. He understood the most fortunate times to travel and the safest routes to take. Unfortunately, he would be away for months. For him, time did not matter. Besides his cabin mate, Razzle the cat, there was no one to come home to. Grimy and disheveled, he would rather never wake up again than live with the pain of his past.

Waking up was just what Jandar did when Zuna started barking outside the cabin. "Jandar, your 'best friend,' is going crazy again," Razzle said.

"I get the joke. Zuna's not my 'best friend' because she's a dog," Jandar moaned. "She's my best friend because she's actually helpful and doesn't dedicate every waking second to being a smart-ass."

"Hey now, I don't like being a cat any more than you like talking to one. Besides, I let you sleep. You promised that if I house-sat for you, you would take me to get this stupid curse removed."

"I did. And I will. Have I ever broken a promise?"

Razzle sat still, refusing to answer as the giant dire wolf noisily ran around in circles. Then she excitedly leaped at the front door and scratched at the knob.

"I'm up." Jandar, holding his head, squinted as he searched for his other boot. He opened the door and watched the large dark blue dire wolf jump upward. The sun was beating down on them, and Jandar couldn't clear his blurry vision. After two days of drunken slumber, the daylight left him momentarily blind. His eyes beady and his hands covering his brow, he strained to see what was above him. He heard them before he saw them. His mouth opened, but no words came out. Overhead streamed dozens of golden wrens stretched across the sky.

It shook Jandar sober. He thought about the aging letter secured with a ribbon and a seal, tucked away in his dresser drawer. "Sorry, Razzle. Family first. Looks like you'll have to wait a little longer for that favor."

CHAPTER
Two

THE VENGEANCE SEEKER

Azoria was hungry. She hadn't eaten since the night before the attack. She pushed the growing stomach growls out of her mind and refocused on the task. She reminded herself that this starving pain was nothing compared to the torture inflicted on her father. His screams had been seared into her mind as she imagined the orcs beating him and leaving him for dead. He must have put up one hell of a fight. Those thoughts made her press forward like an unwavering predator stalking through dangerous landscapes.

It was relatively easy for her to follow one of the groups of orcs. They weren't very stealthy, and their lack of worry reflected their lack of respect for any possible threats in the forest. They left trash, animal scraps, and smoldering campfires wherever they walked. They moved fast, just out of Azoria's sight. She wasn't much of a tracker, and when the rains unintentionally covered their tracks, Azoria led herself astray.

She mistakenly trudged through the neck-deep dark waters of the swamplands. She screamed, traumatized by the horrors of slimy black creatures attaching to every one of her limbs. Attempting to pull off the first one, she found its little teeth refused to detach itself from her skin. The more she pulled, the more she bled. Blood flowed from her arms, then her legs. Seeing her wounds bleed out created hysteria. After the hysteria came the crying. Within time, Azoria could sit and breathe until a wave of calmness overcame her. Soon, she discovered that her fingernails were the perfect tools for removing the leeches as she pinched each one off. Reminded of her hunger, Azoria stared at their fat bodies stuffed with her blood. It was sickly morbid how her anger transitioned to jealousy of the little bloodsuckers. She had no problem trading her hunger for rage. Like the leeches, she fed on it.

That had always seemed to set her apart from the other elfins. While other females drew to traditional family roles, Azoria veered to the action. She never quite grasped the art of peaceful resolution through conversation. She would rather succumb to the simplicity of anger. Again, her temper consumed her, the way the mud covered her clothes and soaked into her sore, bloody feet. It was an easy solution to many of her problems. Often, Azoria confused her anger for bravery. Under the bravado and bold talk lay the deepest part of her: fear.

That bravery was tested when she exited the swamps and entered the Forests of the Northern Winds. As the most dangerous predators sought shelter from the abysmal rain, Azoria continued to trek. Pressing ahead of the beasts may have been the only unintentional scheme that saved her. Even at night, she refused to rest. Merely propelled by her rage, the little elfin trudged through the dark. The trees, empty of their leafy covers, reminded her of the distorted bodies she'd seen at home, with twisting hands reaching out for her. Those who had never traversed the Forests of the North Winds imagined it to be a world of calm and tranquility. That couldn't be further from the truth. The forest was alive and the noisiest situation Azoria had ever found herself in. The howls of beasts crouching on branches above, the wretched screams of predators, and the mating calls of frightful creatures surrounded her. Azoria didn't know what sounds belonged to which animals, but her troubled imagination created horrendous visions. Some animals mimicked newborn babies crying, which she found most maddening.

Within the foggy gloom, she sensed a beast tracking her. Throughout the night, exhaustion set in, and she couldn't distinguish the real noises of the woods from her imagination. That was the same night the adult boar with tusks as long as her legs revealed itself. Azoria had never been more afraid. Nothing was separating her from the charging boar except for a few feet of foliage. From the depths of her diaphragm, she unleashed a scream loud enough to awaken every forest creature for miles. Her alarming scream was enough to change the boar's direction, sending him squealing in fear. Even after the boar departed, she couldn't shake the uneasy feeling of something or someone tracking her.

By the time her adrenaline subsided, she had arrived at her destination. The storm had followed her from the forest, leaving her shivering and delirious. The long days behind her exposed the world in ways she could have never imagined. Stripped of every emotion, all that was left was the rage. It was the last thing she could trust and depend on to guide her. Now, she stood in the downpour of rain so thick it cloaked the moonlight. In front of her was the Boozy Troth Tavern, a small pub on the outskirts of Brightridge. The lights and music set a strikingly different tone from Azoria's despair outside. Rain and thunder became so loud it overwhelmed her senses. Azoria stood on the verge of vengeance.

"Orcs, step outside and meet your fate in the reflection of my blade!" a voice shrieked through the rain outside. Initially, the voice drowned in the mesh of music pouring from inside the bar. A curious crowd looked out at her from the warmth of the tavern.

"Hey, Orcs! You…walking pigs!" Azoria yelled again, that time catching their attention as best she could with the little amount of common language she knew.

The bar granted the three orcs a clear line of sight to a water-traced outline of a small elfin heaving with clenched fists. Unbothered, they remained in the warmth of the tavern, looking down upon the little figure. The music died down, and a crowd began to form behind the orcs.

Finally, the largest of the orcs rose and approached the doorway. "Pay the puny creature no mind, Gortrog," said one of the orcs as he leaned over the bar and tended to his ale.

"There's always someone who's not quite satisfied with our services," Gortrog replied over his shoulder in agreement. He turned and called out to the tiny being in the rain. "Who dares to challenge Gortrog the Dreaded, leader of the Elf Breakers and the chief overseer of the wildwoods?

Azoria's novice grasp of the common language deterred her appreciation of his vicious accolades. She remembered Gortrog as the first orc she'd seen past the creek. He was closer now. She seethed at his rope necklace with fresh clumps of elf ears hanging from the chain like a skewer of skin.

"Final warning. Go home, worm," Gortrog warned.

That she understood. Azoria took in a deep breath, inhaling splashes of the showering storm. The rain pelted her face, flooding her eyes and mouth. It didn't matter. She wasn't there to talk. There she stood, finally facing those mammoths. Her adrenaline quickly drained from her body. The reality was she had no idea what to do next. Her anger had only guided Azoria to that point. Something inside her warned her that she still had a chance to walk away. A commonsense decision to choose safety. After all, none of the orcs were less than six and a half feet in height. Her anger alone surely couldn't defeat the weakest one. *Return home*, the safety mechanism known as her conscious advised. Doubt was filling her. The hunger crept back into Azoria's stomach. The cold downpour soaked her clothes, weighing on every inch of her skin. It was heavy. Her confidence was waivered and that lack of conviction quickly converted into a void of fear. *Return home. Walk away,* her conscious said, talking back like a petulant child. Her inner voice grew from a whisper to a scream.

Return home!

Return to what?

Gortrog went back to drinking, the crowd dispersed, and the music recommenced. Azoria's feet propelled the rest of her body to turn around and walk away, shamefully giving up.

Return to what? she asked herself again. Her home was gone. Her father's body lay battered and lifeless near the charcoal remains that were once their home. *Return to what?* Her mother had died giving birth to her. Her friends had fled to the unknown. She could not know whether Myra, Gymmal, and Sariah had survived. Averstone no longer existed. It was all just a memory. Life no longer mattered. The list of reasons she told herself only motivated to leave even more. *Return to what?*

She'd survived long days of treading through the murky swamps, the thick forests, the old roads, and the wet cobblestones to arrive at that point. Memories flashed of holding her father's hand; the tighter she squeezed, the less he held on. Almost immediately, her anger returned, and the weakness faded away. There was no delineation from where her tears ended, and the rain on her cheeks began. There was nothing now. The anger returned. It was warm and comfortable in the storm's midst. Gripping the blade sheathed over her back, she turned around and made her way up the steps and into the tavern.

Gortrog never saw it coming. By the time he heard her *acha* war cry, a blade of blue tinge extended from his back and out the front of his shoulder. As he looked over in confusion, the other two orcs came barreling toward Azoria. While her age limited her strength, she was quick and nimble. She had no time to recover her short sword deeply embedded in Gortrog. Before another orc could grab her, Azoria jumped effortlessly onto the bar top. The third orc ran around the other side. Azoria kicked a glass mug of ale into the side of his face. Dazed, the third orc fell back with shards of glass stuck in his right eye and ale running down his chest. Gortrog spun awkwardly in circles, trying to reach the sword handle in his back like a dog chasing its tail. Orcs weren't known to be flexible, and his bulky arms restricted him. He had been in plenty of fights, and his scars told stories of incredible wounds. This piercing was different. The sword melted through him more than a stab, but the blade's searing heat was what really affected him. Azoria, in disbelief at her own abilities, slowed to admire her work. That moment was all the second orc needed to pull her off the bar by the back of her cloak.

Azoria fell so hard that the other end of the tavern heard the bang ricocheting across the floorboards. The back of her head hit the ground. Flashes of white light flared across her eyes, instantly obstructing her sight. She was aware of what happened. Her body, however, could not recover quickly enough. Azoria's attempt to scurry off the floor was intercepted by a scooping kick. A large boot thrust into her torso, whipping Azoria into the side of the bar and crashing back onto the cold hardwood. A searing sensation leaked through her ribs as she scrambled to her feet. Azoria realized that her speed was compromised. Now she had to rely on her wits.

The crowd was in disarray. Humans, dwarfs, elves, and tieflings alike all bared witness. Some stumbled into the action to separate the melee. Some grabbed at the orcs but were quickly put down. Others screamed and raced outside to escape the chaos. This granted Azoria just enough time to regain her bearings and assess the situation. An orc withdrew the blue pulsing blade out of Gortrog. Pissed off, Gortrog brandished his oversized broadsword. Azoria managed to position herself at the entrance. She removed the small dagger from her belt strap, her final weapon option. It was no match for her opponent's sword. The large blade displayed a green crystal at its base, with lightning sparks whipping around to the top. The neon green currents actively lighting the tavern intimidated everybody, including the elfin.

Azoria attempted to swing at the charging Gortrog, but the pain in her ribs wouldn't allow her arm to extend far enough. Instead, she could only brace herself by closing her eyes. She didn't want to see what was coming. With all his might, Gortrog front-kicked her tiny frame. The impact thrust her off her feet and several yards backward through the rain, her body slapping onto the muddy ground outside. Once again on her back, a sonic wave of crippling anguish swept through Azoria as the breath heaved from her lungs. She swore every one of her bones had shattered and reconnected incorrectly. She lay motionless, only to hear the thunder above, followed by the heavy steps of Gortrog approaching. She raised her right arm as if it were the last part of her protesting to fight. Gortrog, realizing the unnecessary reasoning for his broadsword, returned it to its sheath. He slowly kneeled and stared with the patience of an owl watching its prey before swooping. He examined the little twig like a curious predator, slowly playing with its dead game. Then, he casually raised the elfin over his head.

She saw it. Her father's gold and silver bracelet. In fact, at least a dozen others were wrapped around his left arm. While her skin was heated with hate, she was practically lifeless by that point and hadn't the will to be shocked. Gortrog was still reeling from his wound. The throbbing pain left from Azoria's blade had only pissed him off more. He let out a yell and threw her even farther. Her body went crashing into the cobblestone street like a rag doll.

She bounced a few times before sliding into a pile of crates. Her nails were caked with mud as she tried to stop herself from sliding further with the last strength in her fingertips. There was almost nothing left of her. The anger was gone. So was the hunger and the pain. This must have been what her father felt as his spirit withdrew from his body. When he became too weak to hold her hand. Her eyelids were the only part of her body she still had control of. She blinked, staring at the moon above her as water flooded her weltering eyes. Slipping in and out of consciousness, Azoria descended into darkness.

CHAPTER
Three

A STRANGER'S WARMTH

Maybe it was the boisterous breeze rhythmically shaking the windows, but something finally woke Azoria. Her eyes were heavy and it took a while to fully open them. The pain kept her body prisoner from movement. She found herself lying in a stranger's bed too big for her. Azoria's first thoughts were to wiggle her fingers and toes. So far, everything seemed to be in place. Her ribs, however, were a different story. She felt the tightness of the bandages wrapped around her. Even if the mattress built of clouds, motion reminded her of lying on a bed of needles. The slightest movement was instantly regrettable. It wasn't just the physical damage but the exhaustion that weighed her down.

She must have fallen asleep and woken up a dozen times. Every time, it was the same process: startle herself awake, check her facul-

JOHN DAZE

ties, confirm she was not in immediate danger, and pass out again. At one point, she woke up screaming through her dry throat for her dad, but she quickly remembered his fate. The thought made her stomach sick. Her tears soothed her back to sleep.

Finally, Azoria had fully awoken. She was coherent enough to realize the unfamiliar setting she found herself in. Scanning the room, Azoria noticed the crackling fireplace at the end of the small cabin, pots, and pans scattered about, and a rope line of drying meats hanging from above. She didn't feel the threat of danger, but waking up in a strange place made her uncomfortable. While warm inside, Azoria could hear the wind howl its ghostly songs outside. The banging of whatever things the storm carried constantly knocked against the doors and windows. Lightning flashed, followed by the low bass of thunder.

While Azoria was thankful to be alive, there was disappointment. Her attempt to exact revenge had been a failure. She was equally concerned about lying in a stranger's bed, in a stranger's home. The combination of pheasant soup and burning wood wafted throughout the house. She then thought of the possibility that the home belonged to the orcs or something even more sinister. With every bit of strength she could muster, Azoria pulled herself out of the bed and fell to the floor. The sound of the door opening sent her into a panic. With nowhere to hide, she rolled herself under the bed.

The door opened. From Azoria's viewpoint, she could make out boots but not the person wearing them. She was sure they didn't belong to an orc. Unfortunately, she'd become a recent expert on orc boot fashion. There was a pause at the door. She figured the stranger had just noticed her absence from the bed. While Azoria was young, she knew the stranger would quickly figure out her prominent hiding place.

"Where did she go?" A grizzled voice sarcastically spoke in Elvish. "I have no idea where she went."

Azoria remained silent.

"Pity. I guess I'll have to eat all this soup myself."

While Azoria refused to answer, her stomach responded in a large growl as she quickly placed her hands over her stomach. She was starving.

The boots remained still for a few seconds, then continued over to the pot of soup on top of the fire. The sound of a ladle stirring the pot was followed by a bowl being filled up. Then, another bowl was filled. She assumed the second bowl placed on the floor was for her until a thud came from a cat landing on the floor, who trotted over to it.

Azoria lay still, absorbing the sounds of satisfied slurping and dishes clanking. The cat quickly checked that Azoria was still under the bed, then returned to its soup. The smell and sounds had proven too much for her.

"I thought that bowl was for me," she said in elvish.

"Are you an animal?" the stranger in the boots replied in kind.

"No, of course not."

"Well then, I wouldn't place your bowl on the floor. I've made another bowl that's sitting on the table. Eat when you're ready."

Azoria reminded herself of how warm and inviting her house had been before the orcs attacked. Tucked under the stranger's bed, she thought of her own family. Azoria wished to have more nights with her father like the last one they shared together. The missed opportunities to create friendships with more folks in her village because of her short temper, began to eat at her. She was filled with so much regret.

There she was, tucked tightly under a stranger's bed with a curious cat pawing at her as if inviting her out. Azoria responded with a smile, a rare reaction in recent days.

"I'm going to step out for a while. Please feel free to eat," the voice said. "You can leave after, or you can stay another night. Whichever you'd like."

Before the door closed, she heard, "I'm leaving Razzle in charge. You're safe with him."

Pulling herself out from the bed, she made her way to the table of soup. Azoria leaned down to pet the multi-colored calico. "Razzle. So, you're gonna keep me safe, huh?"

"What? You don't believe I can?" a voice replied in elvish.

Azoria spat out the first spoonful of the chunky soup. "*Acha!* Who said that?" Panicking, she realized she wasn't alone. Her head swiveled about, looking for anything. *It's the Asharyins! The demons have come to this cabin!* she thought to herself. Without hesitation, she grabbed her sword. She looked at it as if she was waiting for it to provide some kind of warning. "Where are you, Asharyins? You will not keep me in your prison!"

She swung wildly into the air as if to intimidate whatever it was. "Show yourself! Call out again if you dare!"

The voice responded in a deep, wavy tone. It sounded like a silly voice that adults would use when scaring elfins around the campfire. "Yes! I will remove your blood and add it to the soup!" Then came a burst of comedic laughter.

Azoria could feel her heart beating so hard through her chest that it shook her.

The cat leaped onto the highest point of the sofa, staring awkwardly at Azoria.

"Last chance, Asharyin!" she screamed, the thin veil of bravery cracking under her fear.

"I'm kidding, I'm kidding! It's me, Razzle the cat!"

There was a long pause. Azoria turned and looked at the cat, her head tilted in confusion. Then, her eyes widened as if she figured out the answer to a riddle.

"Demon cat!"

"What? No!" The calico cried out as Azoria swung the sword in his direction and drove the blade into the sofa. Razzle let out a chilling cat screech and desperately scurried underneath the couch.

"Wait! I can explain! I was joking!"

Azoria raised her sword again, readying to slice the cat into pieces. "I'll go through this couch to get to you, demon cat! Explain yourself!"

Razzle's muffled yell carried from under the sofa. "I'm a person! I was a wizard's apprentice, but I ticked him off, and he turned me into a cat as punishment! Please stop trying to kill me!"

Azoria remained quiet for a spell. Her brows lowered, then her sword.

"Yep, I can talk," he said, slowly squeezing out from under the front of the sofa. "I also helped make that soup you're eating. How's it, by the way?"

"This isn't happening. How...?"

Razzle ackwardly laughed, attempting to break the tension. "Easy; I went hunting and brought back that pheasant you're eating."

"No, I mean, I'm talking to you, and you're talking to me," Azoria said as she looked at the sword for answers. There was hardly a blue tinge in the blade.

"I told you, it's a wizard's curse. Long story. Not important. I can explain another time." Her shock subsided, and her hunger returned. While apprehensive, she slowly slid back into the chair.

"Is it safe to join you?" Razzle asked.

She didn't say a word. He watched her as she slurped down the hearty stew. She helped herself to a second bowl and bread on her way back to the table. Finally, her voice broke the silence. "Where am I?"

"You're somewhere safer than where you were," Razzle said, sneering, his little white sharp teeth contrasting with his fur's patchy black and orange swirls. She stared at him for a second. Razzle tended to speak in riddles. This was entertaining for him, and a refreshing break from the usual boredom. Realizing he was talking to a child with short patience, he provided some context.

"You're in a cabin in the hills, outside of Ceresbow."

Her mouth full, she tried to ask another question. "How did I get here?"

43

"Jandar brought you here. He has a thing for strays, as you can tell."

The more answers he gave, the more questions she had. "Who's Jandar, and how did he find me?"

"Those are questions for Jandar. All I know is I was curled up nice and toasty on that bed over there. And when he came in carrying you over his shoulder, he shooed me to move. So now, I'm sleeping on the floor again. And you…well, you're enjoying the luxuries this extravagant place has to offer."

Azoria examined the less-than-desirable interior. It was no matter; her tastebuds now possessed her. She savored the turmeric and sweet potatoes, brightening the traditionally bland lentils. Even the dry basil leaves awkwardly floating at the top were eaten. Soon enough, the child and the cat were chatting. Azoria rightfully seemed more focused on her whereabouts than anything having to do with Razzle at the time. Azoria's deadpan stare reminded Razzle not to press by asking too many questions. She was still reeling from such a traumatic event and was unaware of her surroundings. Soon, the weather had calmed down, along with Azoria's hunger.

"Do you have any alfies?" Azoria asked in excitement. Her demanding attitude temporarily cracked, exposing the young, wondrous girl she indeed was.

"Uhhh, what's an alfie?"

"They're so good! They're like these little sandwich cookies. There's cinnamon, cream, and a bunch of other stuff. They're so delicious!"

"Umm, nope. What you see is what we have."

"One of my best friends, her name is Myra. Her family owns— *owned* a bakery." Azoria lowered her head, saddened by the memories. "They made the tastiest treats. She always snuck me a few. Sariah would always share them with me, so I'd get extras. My other best friend, his name is Gymmal. He could eat, like, forty of them. He threw up an hour later, but it counts. He holds the record!"

Razzle smiled, watching her face light up with happy memories. "Myra's family called them…" She snapped her fingers, attempting to recall their proper name. "I'm not good at remembering, so I just call them alfies. I could totally beat Gymmal's record. I bet I could eat a hundred of them right now!"

"Speaking of weird words," Razzle said. "What's that 'Asharyin' thing you called me?"

Azoria's cheeks were full. She pushed a large gulp down her throat, intensely focused on the next spoonful. "Asharyins. When something happens, and we can't explain it, we blame it on demons." Azoria made air quotes with her free hand. "It's kind of a joke, but the elders told us it's true. I don't know if I believe it. Something about demons that invaded heaven and attacked earth."

"That's pretty heavy."

She recited the stories, brimming with the kind of shaky voice that children have before a good cry. She held it in and breathed slowly. "Oh, how I wish to hear Dad's silly stories again."

"Well, since you asked," Razzle said, overly sarcastic. "I left home too. Not because they died but because I had no choice. My dad used to push me around. He thought he'd 'toughen me up' by smacking me from time to time. It was bad. I mean, it wasn't as bad as having a girl swing a sword at you and calling you a demon."

Azoria stopped chewing and gave him a look of irritation.

Razzle continued. "Anyways, I got tired of it, so I ran away. I was living in the streets of Delpho City, pick-pocketing to get by. Well, one of the guys I tried to pick ended up being a powerful wizard. To make up for it, I became his apprentice in training. Well, I kind of screwed that up. So, he kicked me out and turned me into the ferocious tiger you see in front of you today."

Azoria spat out a chunk of food from her mouth as she laughed loudly. "That's funny! A ferocious tiger? I totally get it!"

Razzle was somewhat offended by her absurd outburst, yet also proud of himself that he had made her laugh. He figured it was better than being swung at by an angry elf child.

"I was lost in the woods. Do you know how scary it is for a cat to be stuck in the woods? Anyways, some giant wolf found me. I thought she was going to eat me. I came to find out she was with Jandar. He offered to let me stay here until he found someone to help remove this curse. It's been a few months."

"That's a long time."

"You're telling me? If cats age seven years for every human year, then I don't even want to think about it!"

Azoria smirked. "Okay, how old are you?"

"How old are you?"

"I asked first."

"Fine. I'm thirteen. You?"

"I'm twelve."

"Wow. Cool."

Razzle's refreshing humor and entertaining story snapped Azoria from her spell of sadness. Her stomach was satisfied, but her thirst felt insatiable. Then, her eyes grew big at her next target. She reached over to a mug on the other side of the table. As she took the mug to her lips, Razzle yelled, "That's ale!"

Azoria instantly felt the burning sensation of the cold, bubbly liquid. Yet, she was so thirsty that she followed through. She gulped down the entire mug of fizzy drink. The dehydration left her throat so dry that it made its way into her voice when she spoke. Wiping the foam from her upper lip with her sleeve, she said, "So what, I'm parched!"

"Suit yourself. I'll just let you explain to Jandar that you drank the last of his favorite ale." Razzle leaped from the table and over to the bed.

"I'm not staying long enough to tell him," Azoria said confidently. She looked over and recognized her sword in its alloy scabbard. She was full of hardy soup and an unexpected ale buzz. While still in pain, Azoria already felt her energy replenishing. She leaned against the table to stand up. Her right hand wrapped over her sensitive ribs as if to protect them. She limped to the leather chaise near the fireplace and painfully tossed her cloak over her head. She then strapped her sword over her back. Lastly, she felt her sapphire necklace across her neck to ensure it was still there.

"You never said you were leaving," the calico-colored Razzle said.

Azoria, still strapping her hood below her chin, sarcastically responded. "You never asked."

"So, where you gonna go?"

Azoria stopped near the door. "Listen, cat-face. I don't know you, and I don't know this 'Jandar.' I'm not staying here. I have things to do and orcs to kill!"

"Orcs?" Razzle bellowed with laughter. "I'm sure they tremble in fear when they see you coming!"

"Shut up! What do you know anyways, cat-face!"

Razzle shook his head.

She continued. "Besides, what's here for me? I won't sit in this place with strangers when those I love are dead!"

Razzle tried to apply a bit of common sense. "Okay, let me make this simple. You, little. Orcs, big. Outside, scary. Inside, warm; safe."

As Azoria opened the door, she looked back at Razzle. "Nowhere is safe. Not even here, cat-face."

"I think that's the ale talking." Razzle circled on top of the bed and nestled down. "Before you leave, think about the fact that you almost died out there last time. Without the big guy watching over you, I don't think you stand much of a chance out there. But suit yourself."

Azoria had yet to know where she was going or what she was doing. But she knew it was possible that her friends were out there somewhere. She missed Myra, Gymmal, and Sariah. They were inseparable. In fact, it had only been a couple of days, and this was the longest they'd been apart. Still, something felt comforting in this stranger's cabin. It felt familiar. She didn't know who he was, but a sixth sense told her it was safe. Regardless, her heart was with her friends, and her mind told her to find them.

When she faced forward, a tall figure was standing at the doorway. He towered over her. His silhouette intimidated and surprised Azoria. His scruff scattered over his stone-cut chin, and his hood-capped head made his face hard to see. His hands were at his sides, one holding onto a small barrel. A bow strap crossed his chest, and arrow quivers protruded from behind his left shoulder. He was unfamiliar, but seeing him standing there gave her déjà vu. An odd connection with someone she'd never met. Maybe it was his scent or the way he stood in front of her. It was as if something like this involving the stranger had happened before.

She spent no time getting a good look at him, however. With an overdramatic shove, she pushed him out of the way. As a sturdy gentleman, he could have easily stood his ground like an oak tree, yet he gave no resistance.

"Happy trails," Razzle said. The tall man, Jandar, threw him a stern look of disappointment.

"What?" Razzle said in defense. "She started it."

CHAPTER
Four

UNHOLY SHELTER

While it was cold, it wasn't as chilly as the week since Azoria left the ashes of Averstone. The hilly forest was still wet, but she was able to stay on her feet as she trotted down. The sun was a welcomed change, breaking through the bumpy gray clouds. After a while, Azoria started second-guessing her hasty decision to leave the cabin's warmth. Even if she wanted to, she couldn't find her way back. She was on her own again.

She recalled a few things her father had taught her. He'd educated her on timekeeping and navigation by watching the sun and star's positions. *Follow Tira'Sora's lights*, he'd say. This, however, was an entirely different situation. Firstly, she needed a point of reference, which she had none. Secondly, Azoria never trained under duress. Once again, Azoria allowed her emotions to cloud good judgment. It was anger that drove her to exit the comfort of a welcoming stranger's home for the cold, harsh world outside. Her focus was to find shelter before the incoming night. The ale's buzz wore off, and hints of desperation settled in.

There were a few homes sprinkled throughout her hike. She wondered whether she should ask for help but decided to continue. The little bit of sun the clouds allowed was now fading from the night sky. *At least it isn't raining*, she thought. Azoria discovered a small freshwater stream that ran down the hill. She was uncertain, however, whether the water was clean. She didn't know the process of purifying water, and Azoria would take no chance despite her desperation. Instead, she followed the stream's path, hoping it would eventually lead to a larger body of water. It may be possible that other villages or towns populated water sources.

As the sun set, Azoria wished for another night in the warm cabin. A place to take shelter from the impending cold. Azoria thought about her home in Averstone and how well she'd been cared for. Her hike had given her time to reflect on many of her regrets, specifically how she'd treated her father. If only she could hug him. The cold was setting in, and the aches returned. She just needed a break. Her thoughts were shattered when she noticed the creek she'd been following for several hours had come to a muddy end. It was the moment she stopped walking, calmly sat down, and began sobbing.

"This is stupid! Why is this happening to me? Whoever you are, Tira'Sora, who protects us from the skies. And whoever you are that creates the trees, the rivers. You have forsaken me! You have taken everything from me! You wish for my death! If so, do it quickly!"

Her body shook uncontrollably. "I hate you! I hate this! I have nothing!"

Her wailing continued until there were no more tears left to release. The pouty little girl within her she tried so hard to contain finally poured out like the rushing stream under her feet. She closed her fists and banged them against her thighs. After a few minutes, her wailing subsided into the soothing hum of a song her father would sing to her when she had difficulty falling asleep. Gradian called it 'Azoria's Song.' It was a traditional lullaby, but it calmed her. Amidst her humming, she suddenly heard wind chimes in the background. The sweet clinging of the chimes harmonized with her humming. Noticing the dings, she stopped humming. The chimes stopped as well. She wondered if her humming had activated the chimes. Then, a soft voice called from the forest.

Embarrassed that someone may have heard her, she climbed over a small bank to discover a tiny cottage. The cottage was beautiful, with bright colors complementing the sublime forest scenery. Carefully stepping out from the cottage, an old lady hunched over in modest garbs squinted to get a look at Azoria.

"Are you okay, dear? Are you the one making all that noise over there?"

Azoria stared back blankly. She rubbed her eyes in disbelief.

"Dear, what are you doing out here? The night is no place for children."

The old lady standing at the entrance of her cottage looked up at the night. By then, the clouds had dispersed, gifting Azoria a refreshing view of the stars. The cadences of crickets, frogs, and other creatures could be heard competing for a soundscape.

"I... I don't know where I'm at," Azoria said.

The old lady pointed across the stream. "If you go that way for a few hours, you may make it to Brightridge. You may make it there by the time the sun rises."

Azoria shook her head in defeat. "I'll never make it that far." She looked down in a shrugging motion and kicked a small rock while reluctantly stepping away in the direction she pointed to. As Azoria looked into the darkening forest, a piercing set of red eyes stared back at her in the distance. She had no intention of knowing who or what those eyes belonged to. Those eyes immediately convinced her to go with the old lady.

"Young lady, I'm not much for company, but if you prefer to wait until daylight, you can rest here," the old lady offered.

Azoria felt instant relief. Part of her had been wishing someone would help her again. She'd learned her lesson and was not about to make the same mistake again. In the cold, malignant woods, comfort was a challenging goal to achieve.

The old lady waved to her. "I have no weapons and expect guests to leave theirs outside my home. You can place it at the doorstep before you enter."

"I'm sorry, ma'am, but I can't leave my sword. It's my only belonging."

"Suit yourself, missy." The old lady walked into her home. "Stay outside with your toy, then. I couldn't care less."

Before she swung the door closed, Azoria rushed up the porch to the door and dumped her sword. The wind chimes she heard earlier dangled above the porch's gable roof. She just made it into the warm home. The old lady turned toward her. She untied her headscarf, exposing her streaks of thin, gray hair. Her nose was long, and her skin was worn with deeply cracked wrinkles. With a severe hunchback, she was shaped like a hook, at near eye level with the little elf.

"I'm Azoria," the elfin introduced herself in appreciation. "Thank you so much."

"You're quite welcome. We don't get visitors much through here," the lady said. "Would you like something warm to drink? I have fresh water, tea, and milk."

"Ummm...tea, please."

Azoria studied the old lady. Even though she'd never seen one, Azoria figured the old lady was human. She had always been told to stay away from them. To the wildwood elves, humans were no better than orcs. But this one appeared to be kind. Azoria accepted the risk of engaging with the old human. Under the circumstances, Azoria would trust a talking cat for comfort.

The old lady's home was tidy. Azoria could smell sweet lavender in the air as the lady lit a few candles near the windowsill. The light of the flames swayed among the ceiling, extending their shadows across the cabin. There wasn't much to that humble cottage. There looked to be a bed in the corner, a few stools, and an elongated sofa in the center. The clinking of a teacup and saucer made its way to Azoria. The lady sat across from her.

"Thank you again, ma'am," said Azoria.

The lady, her mouth wide open as if looking for the right words to respond, simply nodded. She moved slowly and displayed every trait of her age with shaky hands and a sweet voice. *Maybe humans aren't too bad after all*, Azoria thought.

"What are you doing out here all alone?" she asked.

Azoria would agree that she had been terrible at making friends lately. She didn't want to make this little old lady feel as if she wasn't appreciative. Azoria also felt as if there was so much she wanted to say that she'd held in for so long. She just wanted to tell anybody willing to listen to her recent adventures.

"Orcs attacked and killed my father. I traveled across the swamps, the forest, and into town to fight them."

"Oh, dear. I'm sorry to hear of your father. But orcs are dangerous. What did you do?"

Azoria tried to explain everything she could remember. Whatever she described overflowed with embellishments. She explained how she'd been able to strike down two of the orcs. The third one had run away. One of the orcs, close to death, had begged for his life. But Azoria had denied him his wish. She'd stood over him and stared into his eyes as she pushed the blade of her sword deep into the heart of the dying orc. Of course, this was all a lie. From Azoria's perspective, it was a reasonably believable story. To an adult, however, it was purely a child's imagination running rampant.

"That's great, dear. Such an amazing story!" the lady said as she clapped her hands. Her excitement encouraged Azoria to continue. She exaggerated her run-in with the boar in the forest. The swamp water became quicksand, which she'd been able to pull herself out of. Finally, she told of the story of a dangerous man who'd attempted to kidnap her and bring her to his cabin to have his way with her. But she'd also struck him down and had been alone ever since.

The little old lady was delighted and entertained at Azoria's tales. She laughed at each joke and whooped at every dangerous twist. "Oh, my dear, you are an impressive little thing, aren't you!"

"Yes, ma'am! But I am no little thing! I am a fighter. A warrior!" Azoria leaped up and pretended to have her sword in her hand, battling enemies at every turn.

"And your father... He would have been so proud, dear."

"Yeah, I think he would." Azoria returned to a tragic reality.

"When he died, where were you?" asked the lady.

The memories unexpectedly hit Azoria like slipping in the snow. She cried out again. With her face in her hands, she felt a small, warm hand on her knee to comfort her.

"This is not your fault, dear," the old lady assured her.

Azoria calmed herself down.

"I do have a question, though. If you are so strong, and you defeated so many enemies, why didn't you stop the orcs from killing your father?"

Azoria's sniffling ceased. The question hit her like another splash of cold water. I... I...couldn't."

"You couldn't, or you wouldn't?"

Azoria froze in confusion. "What do you mean?"

The old lady leaned forward and smiled. "Pay me no mind, dear, but if you would have done something—anything—your father would still be alive."

Azoria scooted her knee back. "I couldn't. The orcs, they were too strong."

"But I thought you fought them at the tavern. Didn't you easily defeat them?"

"I did, but—"

"No, you didn't."

Azoria rose and dropped her cup in the process. The cup shattered into several pieces as the tea ran across the floorboards. The tea looked to be of a dark, thick substance. "I'm not lying, ma'am! I slayed the orcs! I betcha their bodies still lie in the streets!"

A soft chuckle crept from the old lady. "Do you lie to everyone? Is that why your mother died giving birth to you? Maybe she couldn't stand being around such a liar, dear."

Azoria looked for somewhere to escape, but her curiosity planted her where she was standing. "I'm not sure what you're getting at, but I don't like it."

The old lady's laughter grew so loud that Azoria couldn't hear her own thoughts. Azoria's mind was clouded with various events that had taken place over the last few days. Her feelings of panic alerted her to leave immediately. But just like the morning her father had died, she was essentially frozen. Like when she'd battled the orcs, she froze. The old lady's laughter screeched into cackling. The liquid from the broken teacup began to stretch upward into shiny, chromatic fingers.

"I'm sorry, ma'am!" Azoria tried to shout above the cackling. "I should probably go!"

Something dripped on her shoulder. She looked up at the ceiling, which was covered in the same substance that was crawling on the floor. The shiny black goo fell in giant clumps as the ceiling warped and bent. The old lady stood up, rising from her hunch to standing tall. Her arms and fingers elongated. Her shadow covered the entire house as a rush of air blew the door open. The old lady's mouth stretched as her cackling increased into a high-pitched scream.

Azoria cautiously inched toward the door, her eyes fixed on the old lady. She was careful not to break contact with her.

The old lady's voice dropped to a deep tone. "You're not leaving yet, are you? We're just getting acquainted."

Finally, near the door, Azoria zipped quickly outside. Gaining speed, she reached out her hand and snatched her sword. Above, the chimes violently clashed until they mutated into black tentacles, lashing down at her. They whipped about as little Azoria sprinted away. She screamed in fear at whatever that lady-creature was following her outside. Azoria refused to look back. Fear fueled her scrawny legs as much as possible, running back into the forest's black void.

It was too dark. Even with her innate darksight ability, Azoria couldn't distinguish the trees in front of her from the gloom of night. Now running at full speed, Azoria was interrupted by the uneven earth, tripping over rocks. Branches raked across her face. She lost her footing on an embankment, which she never saw. Azoria rolled down until she crashed into a thorny bush. She could feel blood trickle from a fresh gash on her arm.

Then there was silence. The blade grew brighter and hotter. The ringing sound returned. She quieted her deep breathing and withdrew her sword. Its blue hue radiated even brighter in the encompassing darkness. The illumination impaired Azoria's vision against the murky depth of the night. She opened her eyes as wide as she could, to no avail.

"I don't know what you want! Please leave me alone, and I might let you live!"

A deep voice reverberated across the trees. Then a familiar song flowed around her. It was the hum of a song Azoria's father would hum to her. The song she used to soothe herself at the stream's edge. "Little girl, I want nothing except your soul. I can taste your fears in the air. I haven't eaten in so long, and I'd appreciate your succor in the matter."

With Azoria's right arm wildly shaking, she knew it had cut her open rather deep. She swung the sword as if to display some sign of defiance against the creature. The blade flashed streaks of neon blue. Its heat was beaming too intensely for Azoria to manage.

A wretched figure screamed as it flew overhead. Azoria ducked in alarm. She doubted how long she could hold up the sword. Behind her, a thud dropped from the sky. She turned to see whatever the old lady had transformed into.

"Feed me!" it cried out.

Brilliant white light exuded from its deformed eyes and shot across the dark. Azoria thought she could get to the giant boulders for protection. Before she could run for it, the thing lifted off the ground and screeched by her. Whatever this creature was, it was fast. Almost too fast for Azoria to keep track of. Long twisted fingers launched toward Azoria, catching her left arm and sending her stumbling to the ground. Azoria lost hold of the sword, which landed a few feet opposite of the boulders. Caught in between, Azoria had to make a decision. Her left arm was suddenly in as much pain as her right. The throbbing of her bruised ribs had returned.

The thing circled back in Azoria's direction and was increasing speed. They both sprinted toward the sword. With Azoria's back to the thing, she slid forward to make contact with her blade. She grabbed her sword and rolled onto her back, narrowly missing the next attack. Overhead, the thing raised itself upward and descended toward her. Azoria, still on her back, raised her sword at it. But Azoria's grip was weak, and she didn't possess the strength to inflict any meaningful damage. The creature's third dive from the sky would mean certain death for Azoria.

As the thing swooped down, something appeared and leaped after it. The outline of the red-eyed creature seemed to be a giant blue wolf. In mid-air, it caught the thing with its teeth, and they came crashing to the ground together. The wolf rolled off its back and into an attack stance. The wolf was not focused on Azoria, who was now scrambling to get back on her feet. The wolf was much larger than Azoria. The wolf's ears shot straight back, aligned with its tail, her haunches ready to spring forward. A sudden whipping sound sliced through the air above Azoria. As she looked up, she could see another figure behind her in the trees, perched on a high branch.

"Be gone, hag!" a familiar voice said.

The hag-thing looked at the gigantic dire wolf and leaped up. It twisted itself onto a tree branch across from the perched figure. It leaped across the air toward him.

Jandar? Azoria thought. The moonlight traced an outline over the perched figure, now standing with a bow in hand. He released two arrows at once, whizzing toward the hag. She absorbed the arrows and crashed into Jandar. Azoria had no way of helping, as the lowest branch was too tall for her to reach. All she could do was watch in awe as Jandar kicked the hag away and swung onto the branches below him.

The hag raced after. Jandar sprung across each tree branch like an acrobat. As the hag caught up, Jandar dropped to the ground. When he landed, a large rock he'd stepped on sank into the ground. The hag was just inches from Jandar as a rope net shot up between them. The net wrapped around the hag. The hag screeched in anger. The combined weight of rocks tied at the ends of the net was heavy enough to keep her flightless.

"Jandar, how did you…" Azoria paused. She couldn't make out his face, but she knew who it was. She felt a sense of safety in his presence. "Thank you." Azoria wept.

"Thank you! Thank you!" the screaming hag mocked in a high-pitched squeal. Jandar looked down into the hole. The body of a little old hag struggled from under the netting. "You." She pointed her shaky hand up toward him. "I've seen you before." The hag focused on Jandar's eyes. "I can't taste any fear in you. Agony and guilt, you have plenty of. But no fear. You hide it well, ranger!"

Jandar fiddled through his quivers, eventually choosing one. The arrowhead looked like glass, the same kind as Azoria's sword.

"I'm not the one facing death, hag." He pulled back on his bow.

She laid still and sneered. "Oh, it's coming for you. I can smell it. When it does, I'll be on the other side, waiting…"

Jandar released the arrow. It pierced through her head, bursting into flames. A bright white ring of light flashed out of the explosion. Jandar stood unshaken, watching as the hag's body disintegrated into ash.

"Asharyin." Azoria trembled in both fear and amazement.

CHAPTER
Five

CALM & CHAOS

They walked back to Jandar's cabin in awkward silence. Azoria's demeanor contrasted from her rage-injected hike when she'd departed Averstone. She was still trying to make sense of what had just happened. Never had she experienced wickedness like the old hag. Sure, she'd seen what evil orcs could deliver, but nothing on a supernatural scale. Azoria was truly lost, and doubts returned to her mind. The silence displayed a rare humility not often seen in her. She felt fooled by the tricky hag, along with grief and shame for wanting to give up.

"Listen, kid. It's dangerous out here. I have no idea where you learned to fight or move through the wilderness, but you're not good at either," he said.

"Well, I've never done either before." She retorted.

"It's not safe out here for children. Especially for those who like to play grown-up. Nothing less than the gods is the reason you're still alive."

"Yes, Sir." Azoria's words were shaky, admitting to her incompetence without resistance. It was obvious to him that she was fighting back tears.

The elders constantly warned Azoria of her defiant behavior and short temper. They empathized with the elfin because of her mother's loss, and her father's reputation, but it was wearing thin. Azoria thought about her father having to visit the elders to apologize on her behalf, accepting the embarrassment of his daughter's actions. He would probably be ashamed of her recent actions. She couldn't cut through her anger to see the pain she caused him. Now she realized it, and she wished to have him here to apologize. She hoped these self-revelations would remind her to think before speaking.

After a while, Azoria asked, "Twice you've helped me. Why?"

He seemed in deep thought, oblivious to her question.

"Jandar." Azoria's tried again, her voice breaking his concentration. "Why'd you come to help me?"

Jandar continued looking forward. "It wasn't a choice, kid. It was a promise."

Azoria had so many questions, but didn't know where to start. It was apparent that Jandar was mad at Azoria for running away and risking their lives. Realizing his tone may have been a bit rough, he softened his tone. "I'm probably not the best company, kid. I've forgotten how talk with a child, especially one so onery."

"It's okay, Sir. I deserve it."

As Jandar made a clicking sound with his mouth, the tall grass in front of them gave way. A large dark-blue wolf appeared. It was the owner of the sharp red eyes Azoria had seen when she'd entered the hag's hut. Azoria quickly reached over her shoulder for her sword. "Back, beast!" she yelled as the wolf stepped forward.

"It's okay. Zuna's a friend." Jandar chuckled, greeting Zuna with a wave. The wolf's ears perked up as she trotted closer. Azoria returned her sword and looked at the wolf with wondrous eyes.

"Zuna, say hi." Jandar showing a more empathetic side, quipped. "I promise, somewhere under all that mud and blood is a sweet little elfin."

Zuna eagerly rushed to greet Azoria like an old acquaintance.

"Azoria, meet Zuna," Jandar said. Zuna gave a chirpy bark as she gingerly nuzzled Jandar. "Zuna is on her own, a bit like you. She was a mom, but hunters took her babies. Zuna almost died protecting them. I found her close to death. It took a few months, but she healed. Zuna's always just a shout away."

Jandar noticed Azoria could not disguise her curiosity.

"Would you like to pet her?" Jandar asked.

Azoria gave a reluctant grin and shook her head.

"Okay, put your hand out."

Azoria reached out her arm and closed her eyes. She felt the heaviness of Zuna's breath.

Her little fingers were tickled by the cold nose sniffing at her scent. Then a wet lick of a tongue washed across her hand. Zuna pushed her head under Azoria's arm, lifting it up. Azoria opened her eyes in excitement and giggled, raising a half-smile on Jandar's face. He saw that it brought Azoria a moment of genuine warmth and security. Jandar gifted her at least that moment to temporarily mask Azoria from her sadness. No joy could compare to what she once had.

The trip back to Jandar's home was uneventful. Azoria was elated to be back in the warmth of the cabin. The door opened just as Razzle found his preferred spot on top of the bed.

"Hey, look who it is! And she's not unconsciously hanging over Jandar's shoulder!" Razzle said.

"Not now, Razzle," said Jandar.

Azoria ran toward the bed, jumped on top, and curled herself up, bumping Razzle.

"Fine, fine. How 'bout *I* move?" Razzle sarcastically leaped toward the fireplace.

Jandar searched for words to ease Azoria's mind. Ultimately, he decided it would be best not to say anything. *Sometimes,* he thought to himself, *a person just needed time to figure it out on their own.* Jandar hung up his fleece, settled across the chaise, and closed his eyes.

DAYS PASSED SINCE AZORIA HAD RETURNED TO JANDAR'S CABIN. SHE kept to herself, recovering from her cough and the gravity of losing her father. Her feet looked normal again, and she was able to stand on them without grimacing. Her mind wondered about, reflecting on her friends and the village she'd grown up in. She missed playtime with friends and felt regret about not appreciating it sooner. Occasionally, Azoria even grinned, thinking about Ollie and his silly friends. She missed them all.

There was nothing more humbling than losing a fight. Worse, Azoria had lost two. She figured it was unfair since her first fight was against three giant orcs. Her second tussle matched her against the nightmarish paranormal entity. Azoria hadn't fought anything before the raid. She realized the desperate need to learn basic fighting skills if she wanted to stand a chance against any threats she may face in the future. Azoria decided that her priority was to search for her friends. Still, reality reminded her to stay where she was for now. Azoria was embarrassed by Jandar's constant rescues that ate away at her ego, and she knew better than to venture on her own again.

There was something about Jandar that made her feel safe. It wasn't just the rescuing, but something deeper that she found strangely comfortable. There was a familiar connection she couldn't quite grasp. Additionally, she had never witnessed fighting abilities like his. He was precise with a bow and arrow. His quick, cunning movements across the trees were as if he belonged there. Thinking back to when Jandar handled the demon hag exhilarated Azoria, and motivated her to want to be as strong and quick as him. He was the epitome of what she imagined only the best harpy warrior could ever hope to become.

Azoria's first steps outside brought the morning sun bright upon her face. She walked to the hill's edge that his home overlooked. She sat at the embankment with her feet dangling and stared at the trees and tall grass of the valley below. There were a few deer grazing, occasionally flicking away annoying little birds pecking at their ears and tails. From above, the forest displayed itself as a beautiful and inviting paradise. But she knew the truth; that the woods hid unspeakable terrors and cold sadness. She loathed the forest now.

Jandar's footsteps from behind her broke her from her deep concentration. He sat next to her and looked off into the sunrise.

"It's beautiful here," she whispered, her voice still raspy from exhaustion.

"Yeah. I'm sure it's a lot quieter than the town you lived in."

It was. Azoria remained silent, daydreaming of her father and her friends. She missed Myra and Gymmal. She certainly could use their support. Azoria would do anything to run around with them again.

"Where is 'here'? And where is—I mean, *was*—my home?" she asked.

Jandar reached down to grab a small branch and began carving into the wet ground between him and Azoria. "You're in the Crosslands," Jandar said.

"The Crosslands?"

"Yep. Your village is one of many in the the Crosslands. It separates the west from the east. If you go east of here, you reach Galvardia, the elven kingdom. If you head west, you end up in Varos, where the humans live. You must not have gone outside of Averstone much."

"I've *never* been outside of Averstone."

"So, have you ever seen a human?"

Azoria examined Jandar's facial features. "The elders told us much about humans. I despise those terrible figures."

"Why?"

"Because they're greedy creatures who destroy everything in their greedy paths. They eat everything in sight, waste everything they can touch, and they can't control themselves."

"Okay. So, have you ever seen one?"

"No, but I guess they look something like you."

Jandar smiled. "That's right. My mother was an elf, and my father was human."

"A half-breed?" Azoria asked in surprise.

Jandar was quiet for a bit. He knew Azoria was naïve to the world outside of Averstone. "Yes, I'm part human. I'm not so terrible, though, am I?"

"I guess not." Apprehensive, Azoria was still unsure what to make of him. She shifted the conversation.

"Why do you live out here? Away from everything?"

Jandar spread his arms out. "To you, I'm away from everything. But for me, this *is* everything."

Azoria had never thought of it that way.

"Why do they call it the Crosslands?"

"Let's just say that the elves and humans don't like each other much. Has your family ever told you about the Great Disorder?"

Azoria shrugged. "Never heard of it."

"It was a war a long time ago. Changed everything. Anyways, this became a barrier between the elven and human kingdoms. Open land for hundreds of furlongs. Kings can't impose their rules here. It's a wild frontier. Everyone and everything that lives here is free."

"That actually sounds amazing."

"It can be. But it's also very dangerous. People will steal, kill, and kidnap in the Crosslands. We don't get many of either kingdom's best. This place is packed with plenty of gangs and wastemen. Many are hiding from the law. No kingdom will chase them here once they make it to the Crosslands. People come to the Crosslands to either run to or run away from something."

"Which one are you?" Azoria asked with genuine curiosity.

"A little of both, I guess," Jandar said.

Azoria could sense the dejection in Jandar. Being so young, she couldn't grasp the weight of misery he carried, but she discerned it. Her ability to interpret his body language spoke more to his story than his words. It was clear to her that Jandar was running, but speaking about it was something he wasn't ready to do.

Just as Jandar was about to respond, the valley before them broke out in action. A lone bear strayed from the woodlands. It was almost as tall as the orcs Azoria had encountered. Its shoulders were incredibly wide, with matted brown hair. The sheer size of the majestic beast left Azoria in awe. Its muscles flexed in the sun, with deep shading over its massive structure's shiny coat.

The gigantic creature was distraught. Blood flowed from its nostrils and hindquarters. Behind it was a large pack of gray wolves. They cautiously surrounded it. The bear swung about, snorting and grunting. Little by little, the wolves nipped and snipped at it. Azoria found herself rooting for the giant, watching it ferociously fight with an inherent will to not die. The bear managed to stomp over one wolf ragged until the wolf lay still. It hooked another one with its claws, spinning it several feet away. The pack took its losses, with several wolves willing to sacrifice their lives for their fellow kin. They engaged, again and again. Each time, the wolves used another method of attack.

Hours passed, and Azoria and Jandar watched from the cliffside like two spectators in an arena. Azoria witnessed the bear's adrenaline wear down. It still had fight left. Its eyes were wide and filled with lunacy. But its body was slowing. The pack finally sat still for a while, catching their breaths. They'd enjoyed the hunt. They took their time breaking down the colossal animal. After a few minutes, they swooped in again. The bear wanted to fight, but exhaustion settled in. Breathing heavily, it limped in circles with two wolves clinging to its rump. Finally, its legs gave out, and it settled down, as if accepting its fate.

An intrinsic relationship emerged between the bear and the wolves. The order of nature remained consistent, as it had since the beginning of time. There was no immediate death for the prey. The wolves ate into it for hours, clearing the backside first and then the ribs. The bear sat surprisingly motionless. Despite an occasional roar, the host mostly remained silent as the wolves got their fill. Even the cute wolf puppies hung from the bear's nose, imitating their parents in preparation for their eventual hunts. Finally, the bear lowered its head and died.

Azoria cried in silence. She felt an uncanny similarity to the bear, empathizing with the instinct to fight against the eventuality of death. She had been beaten close to it. At one point, she accepted her fate. Unlike the bear, however, she'd survived. Azoria swore to herself she'd become stronger, quicker, and smarter. She would learn to become the hunter rather than the hunted. It was her personal oath.

"The Crosslands can be the most beautiful place you've ever encountered, or it can be a senseless nightmare. Death can come at any time," Jandar said.

Azoria trembled, reliving her own trauma. This was her welcoming into this new world, foreign to hers. She felt connected to both the wolves and the bear. Was she the wolf? Was she the bear?

"You can stay here until we figure out a plan. In the meantime, you'll earn your keep. There are plenty of chores around here to keep you busy. Start by bringing the buckets behind the cabin into the house. You can use the water to clean the floors, tables, and windows."

Azoria made her way behind the cabin. There was a large field with rusted farming tools littered about the far-ranging grass. While some crops grew at one end, much of the earth was undisturbed. Down a small deer trail just a short walk from the rear, she noticed two headstones. She looked around for Jandar. After realizing she was alone, she drifted over to inspect. The tombstones were subtle, two separate stones lying over the land, one larger than the other. Surrounding the stones were flowers. Atop the larger grave was a crown woven from palm leaves. The other is a doll formed from the same material. Azoria crouched to get a closer look. It was obvious to her that these modest memorials were the resting places of Jandar's wife and daughter.

The breeze picked up a little, and a few flower petals spun into the air. Besides the mellow sound of tree leaves rustling in the wind, Azoria was surrounded by silence. It had been a long time since she'd experienced true peace. The modesty of the graves somehow spoke to Azoria. It represented a softer side to Jandar's rugged exterior. It transcended what little she knew of him. The little elfin may have been gullible to the world around her, but a mature compassion developed. If Azoria could somehow package and gift them to Jandar, she would.

"I never had the chance to say goodbye," a voice said.

"The last moments with my dad weren't much of a goodbye either," she said.

"Very true. I'm sure we have more in common than we think."

"Maybe. How old was your daughter?" Subtlety was not in a wildwood elf's vocabulary.

"She passed just after her seventh year."

Azoria was a little older. She had just entered her twelfth year. Her seventh year seemed like a lifetime away, especially after recent events.

Jandar kneeled over his daughter's grave. He had a small sunflower he'd pulled from the cliff-side and placed near the makeshift headstone. "We all travel through this world in the same direction and eventually meet at the same end. Friends, family, enemies; we all find ourselves in the same place. It's what the Great Divine says. Some of us make it there sooner than others. But everything has an end. All creatures, all things, even the stars above us. When we pass, the great Divine will be waiting for us. One day, the Divine will fade into the dark."

"Do you still believe in your Great Divine?" asked Azoria.

"I've lost hope, kid."

"We believe in Tira'Sora. She will protect us from the Drojakon. Our faith in Tira'Sora and the other Celestials gives them the power to continue. My dad said one day he'll meet me in the sky."

"Everyone has different beliefs. Some believe there's a god for animals and plants. Some pray to many different gods, while others believe one controls everything. Many humans worship in Stahlmor, the God of Iron. They say he gifted iron to humans to rule with strength. But one thing most faiths agree on is the ending. It'll come."

Azoria clenched her fist. Whether she kept her eyes open or closed, she saw death. It was either from the two graves before her or the visions of her father taking his final breath.

"Life doesn't owe us second chances," Jandar said. "You can't go back and undo what wrongs you committed. Not all things can be made right. The world will continue, and you'll be left here, standing over graves, forced to live with your decisions."

"I feel guilty," Azoria said. "If I didn't take the sword, maybe my dad could have used it to defeat the orcs. He might be here today."

Jandar exhaled. "I don't think the sword would have made a difference. There were too many of them for Gradian to stop."

"Wait. How'd you know my father's name was Gradian?"

Jandar paused, searching for a response. "When you were sleeping. You called out the name 'Gradian.' I figured that was your dad's name. Anyways, that was a well-coordinated attack. They were searching for something. Do you know what they wanted?"

Azoria looked at him with a curious gaze. "I don't know."

THAT EVENING, JANDAR AND ZUNA LEFT FOR AVERSTONE AS AZORIA slept. Under the cover of night, Jandar discovered a large force of orcs marching up the river. Cautiously following the orcs, he watched them enter a vast quarry behind Averstone. The quarry resembled a giant hole in the center of the forest. At the bottom were orcs directing elves in and out of tall caverns. Exiting the caverns were several carts stuffed with glowing green crystals. They shined bright enough for Jandar to see them from the top of the quarry.

Pushing the carts were young elves, moving them from one cavern and into another. At the center of the quarry were several encampments. There, he saw dozens more elves. Most looked like elfins. There were so many imprisoned elves that Jandar deduced that not all were from Averstone. He figured several other villages had also been raided. Most were in tattered clothes and covered in ash and soot.

Observing the elfin prisoners brought empathy to Azoria's ordeal. He reminisced about the time that Janella and Gradian called for him. It was one of the proudest moments of his life. When he arrived in Averstone all those years ago, they handed the brand new baby named Azoria to him, wrapped in blue linen. She was a little thing with unforgettable yellow eyes like her mother. Azoria defiantly stretched out her arms to break through the swaddle. Even then, she was a handful.

Years later, he returned, only to find the same Azoria wandering amongst the bones of old kin. *She lost so much and yearned for answers that I may not be able to answer,* he thought. Jandar was searching for his own answers as well. His eyes swelled with the thought of never again holding his wife and child. Thinking back, flashes of their life together pushed through his mind.

Jandar fell in love with his wife the moment he saw her. He never felt worthy of her heart, but he gathered the courage to ask her out nonetheless. He reminisced about their first date, then meeting her family. He smiled in remembrance of their wedding in the old village. Then, his wife growing the baby bump. How his heart stopped when he held his daughter for the first time. He swore to her that he would protect them always. Then, the unexpected day he returned from an unfortunately long job, he found them. He called out for them when he arrived, eager to wrap them in his arms like he normally did when he returned. There was no response. He walked further into the house, frozen with confusion as he came across two bodies that he didn't recognize. They had been dead for months.

Come on Jandar, think about the good memories, he forced himself. His wife always smelled so sweet, like peaches and cinnamon. He day dreamed of those soft, small hands. They would fit into his callous palms when they walked through the gardens. Jandar would take his fingers and draw an imaginary line, lightly tickling the inner part of her arm, making her laugh. He never forgot that laugh. Just as quickly, the awful memory of the same arm hanging out of the blanket he'd covered her with and carried her to the grave, shattered his thoughts. Her body had turned dry and grey, exposing her bones. He'd squeezed his eyes shut, refusing to look as he carried her.

Jandar was comfortable with death. He had taken life many times and without hesitation. He justified those kills. One rule he lived by was never to harm women and children. It was unfathomable that the very rules he lived by were broken against the ones he loved the most. Finding the only thing he'd ever cared for, his wife and daughter, dead from the sickness, had been too much for him to make sense of. The sickness had been so unforgiving. Again, the memory tortured him; her hand swinging out of the blanket.

They told him the only way to stop the spread of the sickness was to burn the bodies. He couldn't do it. He remembered how much his daughter had grown and how tall she was before he left. And then he'd found her. She'd been nothing but dry skin over bones. Lifeless and weightless. When he'd carried her to the hole he'd dug for her, he remembered how light she was and how much quicker he'd made it there. *She wasn't there anymore*, he told himself. But he placed her down so delicately, careful not to bring her further harm. He pet her hair like he did when he combed it for her. His wife always laughed at how silly he looked being so brawny and combing a little girl's hair.

Regardless, Jandar needed to hide it away and decide what to do about the child. He shook himself out of his nightmare, with Zuna nudging him back to reality. He told himself he was over it a million times, but the nightmares caught him off guard and sucked him in, whether he was awake or asleep. His hand was shaking, which was his body's sign of needing a strong, cold drink. That would have to wait. For now, Jandar needed to focus on the task at hand. Below, the quarry revealed answers. Orcs were using their captives to mine these green crystals.

"What do you think, Zuna? Where are they moving those crystals?" Jandar scratched the top of her head as they peered down into the quarry. "Whatever they're doing, it's something big. Let's move out."

DAYS OF CHORES LEFT AZORIA WISHING SHE WAS IN THE COMPANY OF her old friends. She begged for fun. Out of her pack of friends, she especially missed talking to Myra. Azoria wondered what had happened to her. Had her friends made it to safety? Was her worry in vain, and they'd been captured or killed? It kept Azoria up at night. But she had faith that Gymmal could bring them to safety, wherever that was. Regardless of her friends' outcomes, Azoria was becoming fretful, constantly complaining to Jandar about the boredom of her situation. She couldn't continue to sit around doing chores. Being safe was not enough. She needed to seek out those who'd committed those atrocities against her village. Azoria had to find out why and how she could avenge her people.

One night, at the end of dinner, Azoria dropped a dish. It shattered on the ground, pissing her off even more.

"I'm bored, Jandar. We're wasting time," she lashed out in irritation.

"Would you rather be bored or dead?"

"If I'm stuck here any longer, then I'd rather be dead."

"It's really *that* bad here?" asked Jandar, taking offense.

"What are we doing here, Jandar? My people were slaughtered, and we have no idea what happened. Sitting here doing nothing is torture. I just can't let them get away with it."

"They're not going to get away with it. You're recovering. And we need to get you back to normal. There'll be time for revenge later. But you're no good if you're fighting injured, right?"

Azoria rolled her eyes, sensing that he was pacifying her. "Okay, so when I'm 'back to normal,' what happens next? Are you going to train me?"

Jandar looked confused. He gave a face that was holding something back. She was very aware of his quirks by now. Jandar remained calm, however. But if things became insufferable, he would self-numb with ale. When the ale didn't do the job, he moved on to whiskey.

"I can show you some things, but I wouldn't recommend going on a bloodthirsty revenge mission anytime soon, kid."

Azoria shrugged. "I'm a fast learner. My dad taught me a lot. He was a great fighter."

Jandar remained quiet, obviously contemplating his next words carefully.

"Okay, I've got an idea," Azoria said. "Razzle was a mage's apprentice. Train me, then we'll get a wizard to change him back from a cat. Just imagine! Me with my awesome sword powers and Razzle shooting magical spells." She kicked off an imaginary scene, wildly throwing her hands around. Azoria made high-pitched sounds like she was attacking enemies with magic lighting strikes. "Zuna will be over there biting off the orcs' faces, and you'll shoot everyone with your arrows! Then, the four of us could go rescue my friends. We'll be like a super team!"

Jandar scoffed. "Yeah, sure. Do you think I wanna run around fighting bad guys with two scrawny kids? That's *if* the furball can be changed back from a cat? It already feels like I'm running a damn day care. If my thing is saving kids, I guess, then I'm definitely not throwing them into battle to get slaughtered by giant orcs. Sort of defeats the purpose."

Azoria stared at him blankly. That wasn't the answer she'd expected. It wasn't really an answer at all. She remained there, unsatisfied and waiting for a better response.

"Besides," Jandar said, "I hate to say it, but we have to consider whether your friends even survived."

Azoria shook her head in disagreement, refusing to believe the worst. "If you don't train me, then my time here is a waste!" she said. "Besides, I don't feel like spending my entire life being trained! My home isn't here."

Her persistence annoyed the man. "You're right," Jandar said. "But just know that I'm not chasing after you again. I've had to save you twice. Every time you run away, I have to go out and save you. I'm not bailing you out again." He crossed his arms. "I've learned my lesson."

"Good! I didn't want you to 'save' me anyways." Infuriated, she stomped to her bedside table and overdramatically snatched up her belongings.

Jandar was puzzled. How could he resolve her concerns when he had no experience dealing with such a dramatic preteen? While he empathized with her tragic experiences, he could only take so much of her snarkiness. He couldn't help but wonder how much of this had always been a part of her personality. Razzle placed his paws over his eyes as Azoria stormed about, slamming dresser drawers and cabinet doors. "Here we go again," he whispered.

In the middle of her tantrum, Azoria belted out, "Why do you care so much, anyways? You're not my father!"

A cold silence shot throughout the cabin. It was as if her words had killed everyone around. After a long pause, Jandar sighed. "You're right. I'm not."

Azoria immediately felt a sense of guilt. He hadn't deserved that. This man had endured so much to ensure her survival, practically risking his life.

"I'm sorry. That wasn't nice," she said.

"Don't apologize for speaking the truth," Jandar said. "I'm not your father." He took a second to gather himself. "I guess it's time to tell you."

Azoria looked up at the stout man, who had both faced death and handed it to others. According to the stories Razzle had told her, Jandar had reached the corners of the realm, from Galvardia to Varosia. He'd faced countless enemies over the decades. Nothing shook him, until now.

He closed his eyes and exhaled. "Azoria, I'm your uncle."

She continued to pack her belongings, unaffected by his claim. He repeated it again.

"I'm your uncle."

That time, it got her attention. She froze for a bit. "What?"

Azoria looked up at him, stunned and confused. It was like the world had stopped for a second. She'd heard the words, but they'd jumbled between her ears. It was the most unexpected thing ever said to her. Jandar didn't know what reaction he'd get. He braced himself for a variety of possible reactions. Maybe a hug or punch, but he received neither.

The silence unexpectedly broke. Azoria burst into laughter. She laughed hard, almost to the point of screaming. She slapped her knees with hysteria. Then she mocked him, lowering her voice and mumbling, "I'm your uncle! I'm your uncle!"

Her laughing was a mixture of disbelief and stalling to give him a substantive response. "You're my uncle? Impossible! Is this you or the whiskey talking?"

"I'm honestly not sure, but it doesn't make it any less true."

Azoria couldn't take it. "You're a half-breed! My family would never be with humans!"

Razzle interrupted. "Hey, I have an idea. Try being a little nicer to Jandar. This guy put his life on the line many times to save you! You're acting like a rude little brat. What he's saying is true!"

Azoria yelled, "I didn't ask him to save me, Razz!"

"Yeah, well, he did anyways. You're alive! You should be a little more grateful."

Azoria looked back at Jandar, attempting to refocus the topic. "What are you saying? So, you're like, what? My father's brother?"

"No, your mother's."

"Wait, how…"

"Your mother, Janella. She's my sister."

"How?"

JANDAR HAD NO LOGICAL WAY OF CONVINCING OF HER OF HIS STORY, nor to stay. This felt more like a last-ditch effort, but it was also veracious, nonetheless. He owed her an explanation. She knew nothing of the history between Jandar and the Dash Clan. Jandar walked to his dresser and removed a folded paper. The ribbon that tied around it held a wax seal—the Dash Clan emblem. He handed it to her.

"You can read?"

Azoria nodded yes.

"These are your mother's words."

Azoria stood solemn. Once her eyes caught the emblem, her fluster subsided.

"Go ahead." Jandar instructed.

She attempted to unfold the paper without breaking the waxy, imprinted symbol, but it cracked nonetheless. Azoria was a bit disappointed, but excitement began to build when saw the letter inside was addressed to her. Without hesitation, she read through the lines:

Dearest Azoria,

I pray these words find you well. There is so much to tell you, and not enough time. If you've received my words, then chances are something terrible has happened to Averstone. I've instructed your father to ensure Jandar becomes your guardian. Jandar is my brother. How that occurred is not important, but know that if I trust him with my only child's life, then you can trust him too.

As much as we wanted you to enjoy your youth, this letter's existence is proof that we could not protect you from what is to come. As my only child, you are the descendant of a great Celestial who protected our earth from the Drojakon. That responsibility was passed down through our bloodline. You are the inherit of this duty, just as your ancestors were.

Your time to learn the ways of the shikari has come, regardless of your age. My brother will acknowledge my wish to train you. Jandar will introduce you to friends outside of Averstone. Each will help guide you throughout your journey as you develop your skills with the Klarion sword. Remember to protect your blade, just as it has protected us for generations.

I want you to know that your father and I's love transcends the living world. One day, when your affairs are complete, you will take your place among us in the constellations.

To Illuminus!
Mother

AZORIA WAS ENGULFED IN EUPHORIA. READING THE LETTER MADE HER feel like being held in the warmth of her mother's arms once again. This was the closest she felt to her mother in her entire life. The joy was intertwined with the instructions of the letter that amplified her confusion. Still apprehensive, Azoria shifted her attention from the letter to Jandar. She searched his eyes for lies, but she could find none. "So, this is true. You knew my mother?"

"Somewhat. The elves of the wildwoods wanted nothing to do with me. As you said, I'm a half-breed."

"This is a lot."

"How do you think I found you? How'd I know your name? Your father's? Do you think all of this was by coincidence? Think of the golden wrens."

Azoria recollected. "I saw the wrens flying over Averstone during the attack. My dad must have released them as a warning or a signal for help."

"Listen, kid. This wasn't my first choice, either. Your father was supposed to teach you all this on your sixteenth birthday. But that's life. Let's face it, we're stuck together. I'm all you have left. Heck, you're all I have left."

Azoria slowly sat on the corner of her bed, contemplating in silence.

Jandar continued. "You don't understand how important you are. Just as your mom was. You'll become very popular if anybody finds out that an elfin is holding the Klarion. Not in a good way."

Azoria breathed in deeply. It was all starting to settle in.

"As your guardian, I'm responsible for you. I took an oath to protect you. It broke my heart to see what the orcs did to Averstone. I couldn't get there in time. I had just caught up with you at the tavern. I knew it was you when the sword lit up. Janella told me it only lights up when in the hands of the chosen one. Azoria, I'll be damned if I just let you walk out again. I'm not ready to lose the last of my family, kid."

"I can't breathe." Azoria held her chest like she was experiencing a panic attack.

"This is going well. Just like you planned it." Razzle laughed awkwardly.

"Let me get this straight," Azoria said. "You're my uncle who's sworn to protect me. I'm running around with a magic sword? Yep, this all makes perfect sense."

"I know this is a lot. You don't have to believe it today because I know that someday you will. I'm going to help you. I'll train you."

Azoria lowered her head. If all of this was true, then she had more reasons to stay than to go. So far, Jandar had given her no reason not to trust him. He offered to train her, and her only wish was to find those who'd caused so much suffering to her home.

"Fine. I'll stay. But you teach me what you know. Then we go to break Razzle's curse. Deal?" Azoria said.

"Don't bring me into this," Razzle said.

"Deal. We'll head to Ceresbow after your training in the forest," Jandar said. The air of tension was replaced by relief. It was time for him to celebrate. He grabbed his favorite mug and helped himself to a tall ale pour. Then he pointed to the floor. "In the meantime, finish the dishes and rest up. You have a big day tomorrow. Training begins at dawn."

CHAPTER

Six

SKULL & ASH

The next morning, the duo made their way out to the vast wilderness to begin training. They trekked a whole day in the dense woods, where the ground was still moist and cold from the previous storms. It was a place Azoria was not comfortable returning to, and all the bad memories revisited her mind. She remained calm on her walk, but her fears of the hag and other predators living here shook her confidence.

As they hiked through the wet terrain, Jandar advised, "You need to learn common speak. You can't live outside of the wildwoods without it. Most of the world speaks it, especially humans. The cities can be more unforgiving than the forest. You'll need to speak like the people you hate to understand them."

"Sure." Azoria was breathing too heavily to argue. She had yet to acclimate to the environment.

"Good. We start now," Jandar said in common speak. Azoria couldn't make out every word, but she pieced together the ones she understood.

"Your first task is to survive. You're no help to your cause or others if you cannot help yourself," Jandar said. "You're small and fast. You can hide in unexpected places. Also, you can heal quicker than humans. These are natural abilities you can find comfort in. Use those natural abilities to your advantage. Orcs are large and clumsy. If they catch you, they can hurt you. So, you must remain uncatchable. "

Azoria nodded in agreement.

Jandar continued. "Being an elf, you'll need to harness your darksight. We can see in the dark, but it takes practice. Another ability you can learn is mindspeak. Some elves can talk to other elves through thoughts. There are even some elves who can speak with animals."

"Can you mindspeak?" Azoria asked with intrigue.

"Not with other elves. But there are some animals that I can, such as Zuna."

"My father told me about mindspeak," Azoria said. "He didn't know it either. He said it's hard to learn."

"It's not easy, but you can develop the skill in time."

They continued into the forest until they reached a mossy, shaded area teeming with life.

Jandar said, "Everything in the forest is watching you. It knows you're here. See these mushrooms? They tilt toward you as you walk by. They're protecting their bodies by using their tops as shields."

Azoria looked about and watched as all the multi-colored mushrooms on the forest bed did precisely that. Jandar smirked. "You were so mad, you never paid attention to the world moving around you. You believed you were strong. That was your biggest mistake. Accepting your weaknesses teaches you what to improve upon. In the forest, ignorance cannot be your weakness. You learned valuable lessons in the darkness."

They dedicated weeks working through various terrains. First, the ranger wrapped the sheath of Azoria's sword in deer hide to avoid undue attention. Then, Jandar taught Azoria how to live like the forest creatures. She learned that there were water sources everywhere. One example included unique vines that absorbed and retained stormwater. Jandar hacked into the vines and drank the water dripping out. He explained that the natural world provided more food than the largest marketplace. He leaned to the forest floor and allowed a trail of army ants to travel onto a small branch and ate a few. Azoria reluctantly tried a few, and found them tolerable. They observed the animals around them and learned their behaviors. He pointed out a jaguar in the treetop above them, and the deadly snakes coiled in hollow logs and under heavy ferns. Jandar showed her that crushing pine needles until the oils were released could be used to rub on their clothes to keep the ravenous bugs and other predators away. He demonstrated that different mixtures of mud had special uses, from sunblock to camouflage.

They stepped through the wet sponges known as peat bogs, and the dead earth gave an overwhelming stench of decay. Wading in the still waters was like gliding on a wide mirror. Apart from an occasional mosquito, nothing lived in the bogs. Jandar explained that these marshy areas would lose any would-be tracker. Quicksand could turn an innocent hike into a death trap with one wrong step. The bogs were an evader's paradise, but it would turn hours into days if one wasn't careful.

Their time in the forest shifted from weeks and months to almost half a year. The rains came and went. Then the hot summer dried out the lands. Eventually, the rains returned. For shelter, they constructed narrow branches into wickiups, with their beds raised over branch posts to avoid the threats of hungry ground critters. While not foolproof, it did hinder most things that crawled and slithered from gathering on them while they slept.

One part of the forest contained the plated spike trees. Jandar explained that most armor would be heavy and only slow her down. He taught her that she could peel the bark of the spike tree and modify it as body armor. She had to be careful, though, as the spikes possessed a natural poison that could paralyze a person if it broke the skin.

Azoria became enthralled by Jandar's knowledge of the land. He was a natural. She watched the way he moved about, how he was aware of every footprint left and every sound he made.

"Is there anything you're scared of in the wildwoods?" Azoria asked.

"I can't think of much I'm afraid of out here. But if I had to pick something I don't like, I'd say spiders. I hate spiders."

"Why are you scared of spiders?"

"I didn't say I was scared of them. I *hate* spiders. Big difference."

Azoria placed her fingers in air quotes. "Okay, so why do you 'hate' spiders?"

"I'm just not a fan. Most of the ones I've had the displeasure of meeting, nothing good came out of it. The way they move, it's disturbing. And their eyes, so many of them. There's something about seeing yourself in the reflection. But what bothers me the most is that they make no sound when they move. They always seem to catch me by surprise."

Impressed with discovering his vulnerability, Azoria teased Jandar a bit more. "Well, it sounds like you're scared."

"You would be too if you'd seen what I've seen."

Further into her training, he presented to her a ranger's treasured ally; the spark tree. Full of flammable sap when wounded, the spark tree was easily ignitable. Jandar demonstrated that birch wood and nut fibers combined with sap created a long-lasting campfire. He reminded her not to drink river water near the cities, but to catch the water and drain it with easily-available peat moss as a water filter.

Jandar advised her that insects and berries were not enough to live on. She would, at some point, need to learn how to hunt. Fishing from the ponds and streams was natural to her due to living in Averstone. What wasn't was learning to build nets and spears. By the third day of fishing, she captured a perch with a handmade spear. She stepped out of the pond with the small fish flailing atop her spear over her head to celebrate her first catch.

She learned basic trapping skills for smaller animals, such as rabbits and birds. Azoria proved herself when she gutted, skinned, and cooked her winnings. Jandar reminded her to always give thanks to the world around her for what it has given her. As she continued to learn, she became less fearful of the woods and more appreciative. She realized how much this world welcomed her in, to a point. Whatever she took, she tried to give something back. When they had found a badly wounded marble fox, Jandar helped wrap its leg and allowed it to lie near their camp for a few nights. One evening, a jaguar had returned to complete its inherent task of hunting the fox. Azoria cried when she'd found the fox's remains. Jandar held her like he once held his daughter.

Soon came the fighting phase of the training. He showed Azoria how to create barriers, first by setting traps, then long-range attacks by bow and arrow. She didn't grasp that ability well, but she caught onto the swordplay quickly, as if it was destined. She practiced daily with the Klarion. Jandar wasn't much of a swordsmith himself, but he understood the basics. He shared with her the foundations of striking, blocking and parrying. The sword was rather easy for Azoria to work with. With a quick flick of her wrist, the sword cut through the air in a whooshing sound. The handle, however, wasn't the most comfortable. The silver spike near the crossguard was difficult for her thumb to avoid. She'd cut it on occasion, which had quickly become a nuisance. Late at night she'd try to scrape off the silver thorn with her knife, but to no avail. Lastly came hand-to-hand combat. He taught her to keep enemies as far away as possible and to engage only if there were no other options. In Averstone, the warriors had never taught Azoria how to utilize her opponent's momentum and weight against them. Everything they practiced honed in on her speed, learning how to time her attacks to create the most damage. There were times, however, things did not go according to plan. She'd become irritated, losing her focus and swinging wildly at her target.

Jandar would tell her, "Do not fight out of love or anger. Both are stronger than dwarves' steel and human's iron. Both are the hardest elements to control. They may convince you to do things you never believed you were capable of. However, if harnessed improperly, either can cost you your life."

While the endless depths of the wilderness encompassed them, Jandar and Azoria were both in their own worlds. Many times, Jandar wanted to return home. Looking at Azoria only reminded him of what he had lost. Azoria equally experienced her own moments of sadness and despair. It reverberated through the plants and animals. Her sorrow brought her closer to her new home. She swore its beasts cried with her in the still of the night.

One night, Azoria awoke to the sounds of loud mumblings. She sat up and rubbed her eyes to find Jandar was shaking. What was left in his bottle swished around violently in his hand. It was as if he was engaging in a serious conversation with someone. The campfire he stared into seemed to speak back to him in snaps and crackles. Azoria stood up and walked over to him.

"You okay?" she asked.

Jandar attempted to look up at her, but the effects of the ale weighed his closed eyes. Sweat covered his brow and under his nose. His wet face shined by the fire in front of him. The flames rose dangerously close to Jandar, but it made no difference. He was numb.

"I'm fine, my beautiful Cessa."

Stunned with confusion, Azoria stepped back. Then memories attacked her mind. She had seen this before. Shortly before the raid on Averstone, she'd found her father in the same condition. The hooch in the bottle was to blame. Even though Azoria was young, she'd been exposed to this behavior before. She recalled walking in on her father as he drunkenly sobbed over the loss of her mom. She was aware that the strongest of men speak to the spirits in their cups in search of answers. In that aspect, her father was no different from Jandar. This was not the business of a child, and she felt uncomfortable experiencing it again.

"Cessa, my dear. I love you. I'm so sorry for leaving you and your mom."

Azoria had no idea what to say. She figured Cessa had been his daughter. A bit apprehensive, Azoria chose to go the polite route. "Thank you. It's okay; it's time to get some rest."

"Cessa, I would have done anything to save you." Jandar slipped from off the rock he was using as a seat to the dirt ground as if his body was missing its bones. Instead of pulling himself up, he accepted the spill and settled on his back. "I was so focused on making a better life for you and your mother. I just didn't pay attention. I'm so sorry."

There was a weird, indescribable connection taking place. Azoria no longer saw Jandar as a stone-faced ranger. Hearing him speak to his daughter drenched Azoria with a fondness she had been missing since her dad's murder. It comforted her, and in an obscure way, maybe she could speak to her own father through him.

"Have you spoken to Mom?" Azoria asked, her voice shaky and unsure he'd catch on.

"Cessa, I speak to your mother every night. She is with me always, just like you."

Azoria started trembling, attempting to control her tears. "Are you mad at me? Did I disappoint you?"

"My beautiful baby girl. You could never disappoint me. You're the best part of my life. I was supposed to protect you. *I* let *you* down. For that, I'm so sorry, my love."

There was silence. Jandar was drifting off from the effects of the alcohol.

"Dad, tell me something about Mom," she asked, desperate to retain his attention.

Her request shook Jandar sober. "Your mom was beautiful. Never in a thousand lives did I think she would pay me any mind. Not only was she a stunner, she was the funniest person I knew."

Azoria exhaled slowly, trying to control her shaky breathing.

"Sometimes, it's as if I can feel you both," Jandar slurred as he nodded off. "I'll be there soon, my loves."

"Meet you in the sky," Azoria wept.

Zuna came over and nudged herself under Azoria's head like a furry pillow. She held Zuna tightly as they all drifted asleep.

AZORIA AND JANDAR REMAINED IN THE FOREST LONGER THAN EXPECTed, which was of no protest to Razzle. He had the cabin all to himself and came and went from the window as he chose. Razzle appreciated the peace and quiet, practically sleeping through most of the day. That silence broke when he heard a pair of wolfhounds excitedly rushing through the brush and toward the home. He raised his head from the warmth of his paws. Razzle was never in much of a rush since his wizard master, Callum Boltbeard, had turned him into a cat for his disobedience. However, the sound of charging dogs would expedite the cat's saunter. As he moved toward the windowsill to get a closer look, a large peregrine falcon landed just on the other side of the glass. Startled, Razzle hopped back, his hair and tail raised straight into the air. He gave out an instinctive hiss. They locked eyes. The falcon seemed unfazed by the cat. It bobbed its head around, intensely peering into the cabin. Just as quickly as it had arrived, it swooped off the windowpane and back into the sky.

Razzle inched back to the window. Four figures were incoming on horseback, side-by-side and galloping with haste. As soon as Razzle saw them, one on each end broke formation and trotted around to the back of the home. The two in the center halted at the front door.

"Sir Jandar, are you decent?" one asked sarcastically.

Razzle heard voices. "How 'bout we burn it down with him in it?"

"No, Lord Almazar wanted him alive, remember?"

"Fine. Kick the door down."

Surrounded, Razzle thought to himself. *If those goons in the back cut off my escape through the window. I'm gonna have to run for it once the front door opens. Cat legs, don't fail me now.*

Razzle dropped to the floor. A bang at the front door was loud enough to knock it off its hinges. The two at the front entered. Both were stout humans. One was significantly larger than the other, tattoos covering his burly forearms. He carried a large hammer in his hand. He looked like he knew how to use it. The other came in after, empty-handed. He did, however, have the falcon on his shoulder.

Quicker than the blink of an eye, Razzle shot between the bigger human's legs and out the front entrance. The big man didn't notice, but the other one did. He was creepy looking and dressed in all black attire. His hair was shaved on one side and long on the other, like a one-sided mullet. Unfazed, the creepy mullet man turned his head, looked at the falcon, and calmly said, "Kill it." The falcon launched off his shoulder and after Razzle.

Razzle scurried as fast as he could for the tree line. That menacing falcon circled and squawked several yards above him. He knew he had to use the treetops to shield himself from the falcon. Being a cat taught him a few things about predators; there was no slowing down. The falcon may be faster, but it didn't know the area the way Razzle did.

The falcon brought its wings in and talons out. Speeding like a downward arrow, it barely grazed Razzle's tail. He made it into the hollow of a dead tree that had fallen ages ago. The falcon darted back into the open sky, looking for another opportunity to swoop down.

"Not today, dingle bird." Razzle snickered.

Razzle was just far enough from the cabin to not be seen by the group of strangers. There was nothing stealthy about them. He watched from a break in the foliage as the group kicked over furni-

ture and rummaged through clothes. The two in the back dismount-
ed and started searching around the backyard. The one with the
half-mullet was back on his horse, while the hammer man demol-
ished the cabin windows. He returned to his horse and pulled something from his pouch. Razzle could see the hammer man turn back
with a lit torch in his hand.

These guys sure know how to make an exit, Razzle said to himself.

Immediately after the hammer man tossed the torch into the
cabin, fire erupted and clawed out the broken windows. Within seconds, the roof warped and collapsed. The mullet man raised his arm
to the side as the falcon returned to him. One of the other visitors
kneeled at the sign of footprints. He pointed east. "He headed this
way. Tracks are old. He's not alone. Smaller feet with him. Lighter
feet, maybe a girl."

"I'm not worried about a girl," the mullet man said. "We
head east."

Razzle knew where to find them. If he could get there first, he
could warn them. Razzle turned and hastily raced off.

JANDAR PASSED OUT. AGAIN. THE CAMPFIRE COOLED OFF, AND AZORIA
was bored. While the training had proven useful, it moved at a snail's
pace. Too many times, she found him sleeping off a spell more po-
tent than the most powerful wizards could summon: whiskey. Once
again, she and Zuna headed out to explore. For hours, they worked
together, corralling hares into Azoria's traps. She was so proud of
herself. The three she'd caught today totaled eight for the week. Later that day, they returned to camp, excited to display her trophies to
Jandar.

Something was off, however. Zuna could smell it in the air before they arrived. The bond between her and Azoria had grown
since training began. Azoria immediately picked up on Zuna's worry. "Wait here, I'll check it out," Azoria whispered. She entered the

camp with her sword drawn. There was an imprint in the dirt of where Jandar had slept, but it had been disrupted. The streaks indicated some kicking motion. Next to them were several boot marks. The ash from the fire stretched across the camp.

"Zuna, I think someone took him. They carried him through here." She pointed. While she continued to investigate, Zuna sniffed around for any additional clues. Then something shook in the branches overhead. Zuna growled in alert. Azoria's stomach dropped, unsure of what could be lurking. She was sure she'd be an easy match for whoever was strong enough to take Jandar. As Azoria turned to face the commotion, a calico cat leaped to the ground. It was Razzle.

Azoria exhaled in relief. "Razzle! Couldn't you just say something?"

Razzle heaved in exhaustion. "I...have...no...breath."

Azoria shot a look of impatience.

Razzle attempted to explain. "People...after...Jandar."

"No, really?" Azoria said sarcastically.

"They...burned down the cabin."

"What? Who are they?"

"I don't know. They said something about Lord Almazar, whoever that is."

They continued to look for clues. Azoria didn't know who she was up against, but Razzle provided a description of the group he encountered.

"We need to go after him."

Razzle laughed. "Not a chance I'm going with you. I like Jandar, but I'm not trying to be dinner to a psychotic falcon."

"Fair enough," she said.

Then Razzle noticed something. "Hey, look over here. There's an arrow near the ashes. It's pointing that way."

Azoria walked in the direction the arrow was pointing. There, on the tree, was a handprint in ash. She was confident it was Jandar's. She looked back at Zuna. "Let's go, girl."

As they walked off, Razzle sat down under the tree. Just as he snuggled into a tight circle, the screech of a bird overheard disrupted his sense of security. "On second thought, maybe I should go with you. Someone should keep an eye on you. Wait up!"

The trio traveled into the night. The forest broke into scattered flatlands, giving her a better line of sight. In the distance, a small campfire danced against the night. As she crept closer, she could make out five figures circled around the fire and four horses grazing.

"Okay, Zuna. Four against two doesn't favor us very well. We're going to have to split them up." She mulled it over. The figures looked human. "We have to do this tonight. We have the advantage, since we can see in the dark, and they can't," she said. Zuna lightly sang in agreement.

"*Acha!*" Azoria yelled.

"Bless you, Zorie," Razzle said.

"What?"

"I thought you sneezed. You know what? It's nothing. Forget it."

Azoria shook her head in confusion. Then she said, "Zuna, you start howling when I give you the signal. Just give me a little time to set up. Razzle, don't get killed." Then she headed off.

"So, what's the signal?" asked Razzle, giving Zuna a bufuddled look.

JANDAR WAS SORE. THE ONLY THING HE HATED WORSE THAN A HANG-over was being beaten and kidnapped during one. He opened his eyes to see a falcon just inches from his face, standing on his chest. Jandar's immediate reaction was to punch it, but his hands were tied behind his back.

"Hey, guys, you gonna explain what's going on?" he asked.

"Don't play coy, Jandar. You—out of everyone—should know your past always catches up with you," the one with the mullet said.

"Aren't you guys getting tired of this song and dance? I mean, you're, like, the third group they've sent out," Jandar said, moving his head back to avoid the falcon's beak. "Granted, they sent out four this time, but each time you've failed."

"Things take time," the mullet man said. "You should have known we'd get you, eventually. The king is patient. The python squeezes slowly."

"Save the analogies," Jandar said. "And he's not the real king."

"Blasphemy, ranger," the mullet man said. "And it wasn't an analogy. It was a metaphor."

"Uh, I think it was a simile, boss," the hammer man said.

"It doesn't matter," the mullet man snapped. "Jandar thought his actions against the empire would go unpunished. You can't run forever. You're getting old. A little slower, a little weaker. The king will see you hang."

Jandar coughed. "Fake king."

Just as the mullet man gave a rageful look to Jandar, a loud howl broke the night around them. The falcon flapped its wings in surprise. Jandar recognized it immediately. It was the familiar sound of Zuna. He smiled to himself.

The howling didn't stop. After a few minutes, the mullet man's patience wore off. "Can someone please go out there and shut it up?"

The other two men stood up and walked toward the howling, weapons in hand.

AZORIA WATCHED FROM THE OUTSKIRTS OF THE FOREST AS THE TWO walked in Zuna's direction. "We'll trap them, just like the hares," Azoria whispered.

Zuna continued howling, bringing them deeper into the woods.

"Just like hares. Big, dumb hares."

They locked eyes on Zuna. Both had swords drawn. Zuna hopped out, barking annoyingly. Then she raced into the darkness.

"Are you crazy? I'm not going in there," one man scoffed.

"Suit yourself, but I'm not listening to this all night," the other said.

"Fine. Let's hurry up. This place gives me the chills." They both headed off after her.

As they continued after her, they struggled to see. Azoria was close to them, studying their mannerisms. She'd never seen a pure human before, let alone four. She was nervous, yet excited, with a hint of curiosity. She'd grown up listening to the stories of the selfish humans being known for destroying everything they touched. Elves learned long ago to stay far clear of them. Watching them stumble through the forest in fear did not impress her. They sure were living up to her expectations, however.

"Just a little closer," she said.

One cautiously moved forward, but was no use. His foot stepped into a soft patch. As his weight shifted on that foot, the ground gave in, dropping him off a steep cliff. He violently rolled down, deeper into the basin. The second man stepped back in panic. Relying on his hearing, his ears heard the other man screaming.

"I think I broke my leg!"

The second one yelled back, "Wait here. I'll get help!"

"Don't leave me."

While the two men bantered, Azoria snuck up behind the second one. If she could calm her nerves, it might work. But she had to move fast. The one at the bottom of the hill continued to talk, keeping the other one's attention. That was Azoria's moment. After counting to three, she ran as fast as she could behind the man. He never saw her coming. She slammed into his back, throwing him forward and over the hill. Thumps echoed through the forest as the man slammed down the hill and to the bottom. He was quiet, possibly unconscious.

"Zuna, keep an eye on them," Azoria said. She knew the toughest one was still at the camp. She searched the woods around her for any resources Jandar taught her about. She ripped the bark from the spike tree and placed it over her chest. The sap acted as a natural glue to her clothes. Careful not to touch the poisonous ooze, she covered her shoulders and limbs with more spiked bark. Nearby was a pile of old jaguar bones. The entire skeleton was intact. She detached the skull and examined it closely. Then, she placed it over her head like a helmet. It surprisingly fit, but the smell of rot lingered within the crevices. Draped under the gifts of the forest, she was ready for the next phase of her plan.

"WHERE ARE THOSE FOOLS?" THE MULLET MAN ASKED AS HIS HEAD swiveled about.

"Yeah, you're not the only ones with friends," Jandar smirked. "You're in trouble now."

"Nonsense." The mullet man continued to look around in modest worry. "We found girl tracks with yours. Where is she?"

Jandar shrugged. "I'm a ranger. I work alone."

The mullet man looked at the large guy with the hammer. "Go check on them."

The hammer man nodded and walked in the direction the other two men had gone. As he stepped into the forest, he raised his large hammer over his head. There was little emotion associated with his large build. He was as burley as a tree stump and didn't seem fazed by the mysterious woods. His beefy body broke through any natural barrier in his way. He left a flat trail of tall grass behind him.

"Guys? Where are you?" he called out to the night. In the distance, he could hear the moaning of the injured men. As he followed a small deer trail, he kicked over a thin vine wedged between both sides. The vine released a tightly stretched branch with the spike tree bark. It was a shoddy effort by Azoria, but it was solid, given the short amount of time she had to construct the trap.

The branch swung around a tree, smacking the hammer man in the chest and neck. One of the spikes left a gash. He angrily grabbed the branch and threw it out of his way. He was oblivious to the elfin girl that sat in the tree above him. As he looked around in confusion, Azoria dropped from a tree limb with her sword held above her head. In mid-air, she hacked into the hammer man's shoulder blade with a downward motion. He roared out in pain. Azoria landed awkwardly, dropping her sword. She attempted to reach for it, but the hammer man kicked it away. She looked up to see him over her. He tried to stomp on her, but she rolled away. When she rose, the man's large hammer came forward. It stopped within an inch of her face. He lunged at her as she skipped back, erratically swinging the hammer again. The hammerhead bashed against the tree, smashing a few inches deep. Splinters of casing shot in all directions. He grunted, obviously in pain from his shoulder.

With his back turned, Azoria slid past the dead leaves on the forest floor and retrieved her blade. The blade began buzzing with blue light. The man turned to face her. They carefully circled one another, eyes fixed on the other's weapon. The sword's glow shone on their faces. They swung at the same time. A blue light rang out against the night as the hammer and the sword met. The impact pushed Azoria back, almost knocking her over. He swung again. This one landed against her left arm, tearing through her spike tree armor. Chunks of bark blasted outward, exposing her clothes underneath. The whack threw her several yards away. She was disoriented, but managed to get back up. He ran toward her, wildly spinning his hammer over his head with his good arm. The hammer man was looking for the finishing shot. He swung, but she squatted down. Azoria pushed her blade into his thigh. His blood-curdling scream shook the forest. Azoria was surprised by the cry. It was strange to see someone so big with such a high-pitched squeal.

Utilizing her speed, Azoria jumped between his wide stance and popped up behind him. Then she sliced at his Achilles heel, dropping to the ground. He released his hammer and grabbed his boot in pain. He rolled on his back, looking up at his short opponent in a jaguar skull with a glowing blue sword. A large, dark blue dire wolf strolled to her side.

"Who are you?" the hammer man asked, raising his hands. She pointed her sword at his head.

"I am the avenger of Averstone."

THE SCREAMS OF THE HAMMER MAN BROKE THROUGH THE NIGHT SKY and traveled to the mullet man's ears. Jandar chuckled.

"Who's out there, Jandar?" The mullet man seemed a bit more concerned. The falcon screeched in short bursts. Something had caught its attention. It flapped its wings and shot up to the sky. The mullet man displayed his sword. "No man alive could challenge the strength of his hammer."

"That's no man." Jandar laughed. Just then, Azoria came out of the woods, her blue blade glowing. The skull and shining sword filled the mullet man with fear. "You should probably get out of here," said Jandar.

The skulled figure marched toward the campfire.

"Last chance," Jandar said.

"Damnit! I'll inform the king that you've declined his invitation."

"Maybe the fifth time's a charm?" said Jandar. The mullet man ran to his horse and galloped off.

As Azoria untied Jandar, he smiled. "What took you so long, kid?"

"Who are they?" she asked.

"First, what'd you do to them?"

"They're still alive, if that's what you're asking."

Jandar's head was still spinning. He figured the only thing that could cure his migraine was another drink. He didn't have the concentration or the patience to discuss further.

"Who are they, Jandar?"

"They're just some old friends who wanted to say hi."

Azoria re-tightened the ropes and jerked them back enough to cause discomfort to his hands. "Not true. What's going on? Tell me, or I'm done helping."

Jandar recognized her scowl. It was the scowl inherited from her mom. She meant what she said. The little elfin had just put her life on the line to help him, and achieved the goal rather effectively. "Some crazy human with a hammer was just tried to kill me. I deserve to know what's going on," she said impatiently, standing over him with her foot tapping.

Jandar sighed. "Fine. I did some bad things in Varos a long time ago. The king owes me a hanging, and he sends these hunters out every now and then to bring me in."

"What kind of bad stuff?"

"I'd rather not talk about it, Zorie. It doesn't bring up good memories. But for you, I'll just say that there was a war between humans, elves and drekolites, known as the Great Disorder. I was a mercenary for Varosia. I decided I'd had enough and left the kingdom, but not before pissing off the king. Now, can you untie me, please?"

After contemplating, Azoria continued to help him. As his hands became free, he rubbed his wrists. Jandar placed his fingers over the indents on his skin. Razzle rushed up from the brush. "Is the coast clear?"

"Yes, our brave warrior here has saved the day!" Jandar said.

"Yeah, but they burned down your cabin," Razzle said in disappointment.

"Again?" Jandar hardly seemed surprised.

"What do you mean *again*?" asked Azoria.

"They tend to do that every time they pay me a visit."

Razzle looked around. "Well, no need to stay here. What do we do?"

Jandar exhaled in frustration. "Zorie, I think you've proven yourself to be quite a formidable opponent. Thank you for saving me. Looks like *my* training paid off." He smiled at Azoria as he continued. "I say we take the horses and head out to Ceresbow. Nobody will be looking for us there. I think it's time I took you to meet a friend of mine. She knew your mother, Zorie. She can explain more than I can about our family and your sword. Also, I promised Razzle I'd reach out to someone to help him with the curse."

Razzle's ears perked up. "Really? This is great if it's true. I'll believe it when I see it."

"Fair enough," Jandar said. He watched Azoria as she placed her prop helmet on the ground. "A jaguar skull, huh? Creepy, but I like it."

IN A DARK CORNER OF THE ROOM SAT A MYSTERIOUS FIGURE. HE WAS hard to see, and Colvin could only make out a silhouette. Gray and white smoke danced upward and out of the stranger's smoking pipe, the air scented with fresh tobacco. As the stranger inhaled, the tobacco brightened like a miniature sun. After a few awkward minutes of dead silence, the stranger spoke, the smoke spilling from his lips and nostrils. "Colvin," he said, "my associates have conducted quite a bit of research on you."

Colvin smiled, his hat tilted to cover the scar along the right side of his face. After all, he was the one usually doing the tracking. Colvin was a fast hand in a fight, strong enough to handle the heaviest brawlers. After the Great Disorder had ravaged his hometown, Colvin headed north to find employment as a guide. He'd worked along several outposts escorting travelers throughout the Crosslands. The Crosslands consisted of either mountainous terrain too challenging to venture through alone, or long stretches of valleys perfect for ambush. Decisions related to traversing the Crosslands weren't measured by time or distance, but by landscape.

"We've done our research, boy." The stranger's voice was rough, as if he'd been screaming himself hoarse prior to this meeting.

"And what does your research tell you?" Colvin maintained a weary eye on the two guards in the room; one helping the stranger pack his pipe.

"Well," the stranger said, puffing again, "you're a drifter, once a shadow ranger who ventured out as a wagon hand and guide for several of years. That is, until someone accused you of stealing a royal's property and they sliced your face open wide." The stranger took the thin end of the pipe and mimicked a cutting motion on the side of his face.

"I wasn't stealing," Colvin said defiantly, rubbing the scar over cheek. "It's not my fault his daughter took a liking to me."

"Cute." The stranger waved the guard away from his desk as he cleared his throat. "I also know that you worked with a fellow guide, a half-breed drunk named Jandar."

"Jandar." The name struck him like a bell, and name brought back unpleasant memories. The one who spoke little and drank often. Jandar had been his mentor until a fateful day had diverted their paths. Colvin followed him to war, and to hell. He never saw Jandar again after the incident at Red Bend. The altercation that had left their passengers dead and their bodies scattered throughout the prairie fields. He blamed Jandar for those travelers' deaths and hated him for it. But this was years ago. Since Red Bend, bounties had been placed on his Jandar's and Colvin's heads. Colvin could only assume this was about bringing him in.

"What about Jandar, sir?"

The stranger leaned forward, but was still hard to make out in the dark. "I'm not concerned with Jandar. It's his companion."

Jandar has a companion? Colvin thought to himself. "That's news to me."

"Yes, she's a little elfin girl. She has something that belongs to my employer. He wishes for its retrieval."

Jandar may have lost of step or two, but he surely wouldn't be easy to creep up on. "So, you want me to retrieve this thing? Why can't you go ask for it?"

"It's not that simple. There's a saying, 'It takes a shadow ranger to hunt a shadow ranger'. My employer is very powerful. However, what this elfin has is something he cannot touch. He requires some-one to bring it to him so my employer can have it destroyed."

Colvin considered the offer for a while, still leaning against the wall. "So you want me to go to Jandar and this girl and get some-thing? Sounds easy enough. What is it?"

"The girl possesses a short sword. A special blade that looks as if it's made of glass."

"Must be important to hire me to retrieve it. What about your guards? You seem to have people at your disposal."

"This task cannot be connected to me or my employer in any way. I need you to first find where they're at, then report back to me. Track, follow and observe them without being seen. They were in the wildwoods outside of Averstone. They may have made their way to Ceresbow. Keep an eye on them in the meantime. You'll be directed to take the blade when the time is right."

"You know generally where they're at, but you still need me to keep an eye on them?"

"Yes. I know your reputation. I understand there aren't many who can get the drop on a tracker like Jandar."

Colvin was well aware of Jandar's strengths. He admired the war-hardened veteran who used his experience in tracking and guid-ing. Jandar was a skilled ranger and could easily blend into any envi-ronment. If he sensed he was being followed, it would be impossible to catch him off guard again. Colvin also knew his weaknesses. Jan-dar was a heavy drinker, and coupled with his age, he was well past his prime. His emotional attachments to his deceased family affected his clarity in making split-second decisions, eventually costing them their friendship.

Just when Colvin thought he might get a look at the stranger, the unknown figure reclined back in his chair, deeper into the dark-ness. "The blade has certain 'abilities.'" He hooked his fingers in air quotes. "When this elfin took possession of the blade, she activated it like a beacon. Again, keep an eye on them, as I need to know how she's engaging with the blade."

Colvin nodded. "Sounds good, but what sounds better is the pay."

The stranger motioned to a guard, who walked over and handed Colvin a small but heavy sack. "Half now, half after. Just as we agreed upon," said the stranger. "Are you up to the task?"

Colvin leered. Of course he was. He was younger, possibly quicker, and highly motivated to earn the remainder of the loot. "Who do I check in with?"

"I have friends throughout the Crosslands. They'll be in touch."

"So, you're sending people to watch me watch someone." Colvin shrugged. "Whatever. As long as I get paid."

CHAPTER
Seven

OF BLOOD & BLADE

A zoria's introduction to a city could not have been any more startling. It was a stark contrast to the quiet calm of the forest. While Ceresbow operated like a big city, it began as an outpost for traders before the Great Disorder. After many years of war, many displaced refugees from various regions settled there. Ceresbow was a central hub for commerce in and out of the Crosslands. No amount of insight Jandar had provided during the journey toward the city could have prepared her. He explained that Ceres had been a fierce human archer during the Great Disorder, who took a stand with the elves against his own. Against a human army three times larger, Ceres held the once tiny fort and eventually drove the forces back. That pivotal victory eventually led to the Crosslands Accords that solidified its independence from both Varosia and Galvardia. The bronze statue honoring Ceres and his bow in the town center had devolved into patina and bird dung, leaving it unrecognizable. The town's inhabitants had devolved as well. Jandar had spent extensive time in the city, usually meeting clients and guiding them through the Crosslands.

The kind of people in Ceresbow were either those searching for redemption from their troubles or stirring some up. Azoria's negative preconceptions of big-city living had been justified. The party could smell and hear Ceresbow before they saw it. At first, she hated it. It was dirty. The muddied, overridden road widened to allow multiple lanes of traffic to flow in and out of the city. The ground was like soup, pasting itself to their boots and pant legs. The constant congestion of wagons, horses, and carts ground the dirt into soot, rising into a brown haze in the sky. Azoria and company found themselves in organized chaos. Vendors with tents and wagons posted around the decaying city walls. The crowds surrounding Azoria and her company were filled with more types of beings than she had ever imagined existed. An old man standing behind Azoria startled her with his erratic coughing, attempting to clear the dirty spores from his nostrils. A mom was yelling at her crying child. A small crowd of people were laughing at someone's story. Noise was everywhere. Soon, all the voices around them blended into a melody of symphonic disarray.

Azoria was staggered by the endless population of humans, elves, and other types she'd never seen before.

"I'm confused," she mumbled to herself in alert mode. "How could so many beings from different realms all be together in one place? Especially humans. It would dishonor the elders to see such things."

"Why? Because someone told you humans were bad?" Jandar said. "Not everything falls into the categories of good and evil. Not all humans are evil, and not all elves are good."

Azoria snapped back angrily. "Don't speak to me of elves. My people died for what? Just for existing? *They* attacked *us*."

Azoria knew Jandar was still boiling over the loss of his home. His patience was extremely low. At this moment, she didn't care.

He said in a steely tone, "Just keep your head down and keep your prejudices to yourself while we're in town. I tire of bailing you out because you can't control your feelings."

"As I recall, I saved you last time," Azoria said. To most, Jandar was a somewhat intimidating person. His ranger skills, rugged exterior, and calm demeanor made him a daring opponent for most. Azoria took delight in knowing she saved him. She wore it like a medal ceremoniously presented by a king, and it gave her the advantage in any argument they had. They were even, as far as Jandar was concerned. Regardless, the constant reminders from an obnoxious twelve-year-old girl was a kick to his pride. And she was not shy about it.

By then, Azoria was furious. Seeing parties of orcs walk about confused her. Her defenses were at an all-time high. There was too much to keep track of at one time. Orcs, humans, elves, dwarves; everyone blended into a mass. What could she do? The streets were too busy to remain in a constant state of alert.

A while later, she settled down some. Soon, Azoria's displeasure turned to curiosity. Some humans waved a hardy hello to her and Jandar. She couldn't help but stop and take in the endless motion around her. Jandar would nudge her to continue walking. *Perhaps not all humans were terrible people*, she thought. Just maybe, some weren't so hellbent on destroying the Earth.

"Keep your head down and try to blend in," he said.

"Blend into this? I could strike someone down, right here on the street, and nobody would blink an eye."

"You're probably right, but I don't want to find out," Razzle said.

Azoria had never seen so many people before. Yells from merchants promoting their crafts competed against artisans and town criers for patron's attention. Religious figures preached from pulpits made of crates and hay barrels. All types of musicians and bards entertained crowds. The ear-splitting convergence of noise became so loud that Jandar and Azoria temporarily exchanged speaking for nods and hand motions.

Ruins that were once city walls lay dilapidated, uneven, and sparse. Where the city lacked walls, it was made up with militia members who'd banded together to protect the city. It was challenging to determine soldiers from civilians due to the lack of uniforms. Ceresbow relied on its rag-tag makeup of citizens to form its defensive policing systems. They welcomed all from the Crosslands and never gave much thought to the external factors between the warring kingdoms surrounding them.

The city greeted Azoria with an overwhelming smell of baked goods and cooked meats that hypnotized her senses. Jandar appreciated the aromas as well, welcoming them like an old friend.

"First, we eat!" he yelled over the noise to Azoria as they passed the town square. Finding a tavern with outdoor seating caught their interest. A tavern's interior was notoriously decorated with drunken stragglers and roughens. The last thing Jandar needed was to run into a misunderstanding that could only be sorted out by fisticuffs. The last place he wanted to be was cornered in an overcrowded, dimly light tinder box. Sitting outside, they discussed the matters at hand. Like a stern father, Jandar revisited their conversation during their stroll to town, starting trouble in a big city.

"As you know, we can't afford to get into trouble here," Jandar said for the twenty-somethingth time.

"Yes, yes, I know," Azoria said, shaking her head. Her eyes were fixated on all the actions taking place around her.

"I'm serious, Azoria. We're here for two things. Find someone to help Razzle with his…condition."

Razzle, lying at Jandar's feet, raised his head. "Condition? Really?"

"The second thing is—"

"Yes, I know that too," Azoria said, studying the crowd before her. "We need to find more information on Clair."

"Who?"

"I don't remember the sword's name, so I just call her 'Clair.'"

"Clair is a lovely name," Jandar said. He figured it was best to avoid correcting her. He didn't want her walking around and bringing up the Klarion.

"But keep your voice down," Jandar calmly said, observing the people Azoria wasn't. "You never know who's watching or listening."

As they settled for a square wooden table, the tavern's wench stopped to take their orders.

"Do you have alfies? Azoria burst out.

"Umm, what are those?"

"*Acha*," she said in disappointment. "Never mind."

Jandar, both curious and annoyed, asked, "What's with you and these 'alfies?'"

"Can we go to a bakery later? I can't really explain it, but I can show you."

The alfies represented more to her than just the cookie itself. It symbolized a better time with her friends, Myra, Gymmal, and Sariah. At times, Myra would sneak a few from the bakery to distribute at the creek. Other times, Myra's mom would give them a handful after school. Azoria always refused to share them with Gymmal because he would take more than one. Today, however, she would share all of them just to be with him again.

"Azoria, you keep saying, '*acha*.' What does that mean?" Razzle asked, genuinely curious.

"Oh, it's just something we say back at home. *Acha* is, like, if something good happens, like if we have a good hunt. Then we say, '*Acha!*' But we also say it when something bad happens, like when I stub my toe. I say, '*Acha!*' Our warriors also use it as a war cry. When we go to battle, we yell, '*Acha!*'"

The wench returned to with their meals. She looked over at Jandar. "Would the grown-up like a grown-up drink, hun?"

Jandar's hand was shaking again. It had been a few days without a drink. While the traveling had kept his mind from the thought of alcohol, the urges were creeping back in. "I'll have a thunder ale, thank you."

"I thought you weren't drinking anymore," Azoria said.

Jandar was obviously embarrassed by the uncouth child, but he remained calm while focusing all his attention to the wench. "Just one to take the edge off. Besides, it's my schillings. I'll spend them how I please."

Azoria crossed her arms and huffed in protest.

"The wench picked up on the child's forceful attitude. "Sounds like you need something stronger than a thunder ale."

"He promised he wouldn't drink again." Azoria interrupted.

"Young lady, I'm afraid you're probably driving him to drink rather than stop him," she smiled as she walked away to retrieve their order.

The tension between Azoria and Jandar lasted just until their food was delivered. The hot plate consisted of turkey pie and a cake for dessert. While it wasn't a tray full of alfies, it was a satisfying break from the hunting, scavenging, and preparation for her food that she'd become accustomed to. The meal signified an escape from her realities, even if just for a moment.

Because her stomach was full, she would have rather called it a day and fallen into a clean bed. Her reality, however, was to rise from her seat and follow Jandar. As they got up, a group of elves and humans barreled out of the tavern, bumping shoulders with Jandar. They all wore thick-knitted beige tunics with brown collar strings, derby hats, and red sashes tied around their right arms. Jandar recognized them immediately—the Blood Chuggers. They were an organized crime syndicate that operated throughout the Crosslands. They were loud, boisterous, and cocky. They were particularly dangerous in bunches. Jandar knew them well and did his best to avoid them.

The Chuggers set checkpoints throughout the Crosslands for mischievous activities like 'tax-collecting' passersby. Whatever 'fundraisers' they could create to score revenue were used for hunting tieflings. Those humanoids were hunted down and killed for their horns, ground into a fine powder, and sold as the drug known as VibeSpice. Users described the experience as 'vibrating' in euphoric zeal. The tieflings mostly lived near the sinister realm of DarkEver. If they ever happened to travel into large cities such as Ceresbow, they came in larger groups. Jandar hoped to avoid both parties. Unfortunately, hope didn't go far in those parts.

"Hey there, old buddy!" A familiar voice caught Jandar's attention. Kensey, a fellow from his ranger days, was now affiliated with the Blood Chuggers. Relieved, Jandar sighed and returned the greeting.

"Hail to you, Kensey."

"Hail to you, good Jandar!" Kensey aggressively patted Jandar's shoulders in excitement.

Kensey was just a tad shorter than Jandar. His usually bright blue eyes were bloodshot, and he was unsteady. It was an obvious sign of an ale and VibeSpice concoction. Blood Chuggers abusing the same drugs they sold was a well-known and unspoken fact. While reckless and unpredictable, Blood Chuggers were a coordinated gang, a mixture of ex-soldiers, delinquents, runaway prisoners, and fiends. All were looking to make quick coinage.

"Jandar, here for work again, huh? All work and no play?"

"Something like that. What brings you to C-bow?" Jandar asked.

Kensey overly concentrated on Jandar's words, an obvious sign of being under the influence. "You know, celebrating another successful business deal."

Jandar could see over Kensey's shoulder and into the tavern. Someone was laid out across the floor pretty well. Whoever he was, a few patrons tended to him, with white towels wiping the blood from his leaking head.

"I see," Jandar said with a cautious smile.

"Well, well, well. Who's this?" Kensey glanced over at Azoria. "I didn't know you liked them young, huh?" He gave an exaggerated wink and a stinging jab to Jandar's shoulder.

"That's funny!" Azoria quickly responded, reaching behind her back. "I have a friend named Clair who would love to hear that joke. Lemme get her so you can tell it again."

Jandar spoke over her, rubbing his arm. "Oh, it's not like that. I'm watching a friend's kid until they…get back into town."

Kensey, who'd barely heard him, was dragged off by a few of his fellow Chuggers. "Jandar, be careful going east, okay, my boy? It's getting hot over on that side of the C-Lands. Rumor has it the Varosians are starting to cut up some real estate for mining. If you're still guiding, you may wanna move your ventures further west!"

His words were unexpected. Jandar knew that Kensey spoke like a gushing river in the springtime once he was high. Before Jandar could follow up with a question, several Chuggers got in between them and forced Kensey farther back through the town square.

"Little girl! Take care of that one for me! I owe him my life! He saved me during the Disorder! Best ranger I ever met," Kensey wailed before turning away and tussling with his buddies.

Azoria blankly starred at Jandar. "Well, that was…weird. C-Lands? C-Bow?"

"C'mon, I'll explain later." Jandar cleared his throat in embarrassment.

"That sounds 'C' Great!" Azoria mocked.

"You're doing it wrong."

"Whatever." She followed with an annoyed side-eye.

They walked along the narrow, uneven cobblestone roads in the eastern portion of Ceresbow to finally reach the *Crooked Glass*. Besides the shopkeeper, the store was empty. It was an alchemy shop that also sold harmless amateur magic kits. It was a far cry from where Azoria imagined a place where alchemists, old wizards, and spell users congregated. It was a small, simple shop. It resembled a thrift store, with miscellaneous used items on shelves that travelers left behind. Nothing seemed out of the ordinary. The half-empty isles presented the occasional trinket, some unidentified bottles of liquids, and small, useless trinkets and clothes.

"This is the best magical stuff in town?" Azoria muttered to herself.

"This place isn't as it seems," Jandar said.

The shopkeeper behind the counter saw Jandar. He stepped down from his stool and walked over to greet them. He looked human, but shorter than Azoria. "Hail to you, Jandar."

Jandar smiled. "Hail to you."

"You're here to see Nashara?" the shopkeeper asked.

Jandar nodded. "We're also here to help this boy, who was a mage's apprentice. The mage put a curse on him, and we'd like to get it removed."

The shopkeeper laughed and bent down. "I see. Yep, you don't look like a boy anymore, do you? Well, you know a mage's curse is bound for life. But there may be some extenuating circumstances that can bypass that bind." He examined the calico cat. "So, what'd you do?"

Razzle hung his head down in shame. "I stole something."

"I see." The shopkeeper smiled. "Well, you're young and young people are entitled to make a mistake or two. If this good ranger vouches for you, then I'm certain you've learned your lesson."

The shopkeeper motioned them to the back of the store. He waved his hands and whispered something. The wall he was facing began to ripple, almost like water. Azoria stepped back at the unexpected sight. Through the ripples was a library-looking room with several figures. Some were writing, others were standing in groups conversing. With his left arm extended, the shopkeeper motioned for the party to walk through. "Ask for Darius the Augurer. He should be familiar with this particular spell."

"Where is this?" Azoria asked.

"It's next door," Jandar smirked. "I figured we'd go this way for dramatics. Way better than walking around, right?"

The shopkeeper moved them ahead through the portal. He leaned in closer to Jandar for only him to hear. "The Order's conducting a rather important meeting in there. Rumor has it something's coming to the Crosslands, and it wasn't invited."

Even though he was surprised by the news, Jandar remained stone-faced. "Thanks."

"I was a mage. Don't be scared Zorie, it's perfectly safe!" Razzle was the first to shoot through the wall portal. Azoria nervously poked at the ripples, like when she would dip her toes in the creek to test the water's temperature. She held her breath for some odd reason and awkwardly jumped through. The others followed.

"I think it's safe to breathe now," Jandar laughed at Azoria.

The little man stretched his arms out as they stepped through. "Welcome to the Order Divinity. It's like a study hall for mages. Filled with group thinkers who talk politics, trade spells, and occasionally engage in cocktails. Jandar's been here before. I'm sure he can show you younglings around."

Wow, Azoria thought to herself. This large, busy room resembled a grand library. The space was filled with beings of many shapes, colors, and sizes. Many were races and species she had never seen before. One person was hovering in the air and conversing with someone standing upside down on the ceiling. A ferret with bat wings buzzed past their heads. Razzle assumed it was a wizard's pet familiar. Some were practicing spells, while others worked with beakers to create potions.

The shopkeeper was right; the large group in the center was discussing various matters related to some sort of threat. Jandar overheard talk of a portal and a menacing figure who could change the sky's color. A sorceress queen. Before he could gain more intel, Razzle decided to make a scene.

As the room's crowd of magic users looked over at the new arrivals, Razzle impatiently broke the anxious mood. "Darius!" he said. "Sir Darius, I desperately need your help!"

A tall, slender fellow in red garments and a gold belt sat at a desk. A quill wrapped by his long, fuzzy beard scribbled expeditiously into a book. Standing at his side was a young lady, approximately Azoria's age, holding a leather satchel with several scrolls.

"Well, a talking cat!" Darius said. He looked over toward Jandar. "Lemme guess, you need me to remove this cat's voice?"

Jandar chuckled to himself as Razzle jumped onto the nearest chair. "Sir Darius! I am Razzle. Apprentice to Sir Callum Boltbeard of Delpho!"

Darius the Augurer laughed. "I'm familiar with Delpho. That's near Brightridge. You're far from your home, cat."

"I ran away, sir. I made a mistake."

Darius roared with laughter. "I'm assuming you're not much of an apprentice if he turned you into a cat! What exactly did you do to piss off this 'Boltbeard of Delpho?'"

"I was a great apprentice, sir! I just got a little too handsy with a particular magical item."

"Handsy, huh?" Another wizard laughed from across the room. Others chimed in with side jokes.

"Ha-ha!" mimicked Razzle. "Laugh it up, everyone. But sometimes you work us apprentices to the bone! Fetching your work, days and nights writing, being away from our families for months or even years! We're not perfect, and we do mess up. But we mean well." He looked to Darius' apprentice for support, but she gave none.

"Little kitty-cat, do you know where you're at? And just who you're speaking to in that tone? You're in the halls of the most prominent mystical figures of the Crosslands. Any 'good' apprentice would show more respect by acknowledging the rules of these halls."

"You're right," Razzle said. "I think being a cat has gotten to me a bit. I'm always full of energy, and almost always in a terrible mood. I'd be better if I was back to my old self!"

"That is no excuse, cat." Darius' stare pierced through Razzle's emotional shell. "When you took the oath of a wizard's apprentice, you agreed to the long hours, time away from home, the dedication to our every need. You do this because we have all done this before. Look around."

Razzle looked at the faces across the room, all from different backgrounds, races, and languages. They were there for one common purpose; to appreciate the arts of the mystics. Razzle cleared his throat, reciting something he memorized a while ago. "Magic transcends across people and lands, from orcs to humans, dwarfs and gnomes, dragons and kings. Various disciplines represent cultures and regions, in the physical and mystical. Most used it to better their societies, while others manipulated it to destroy and conquer."

Darius continued. "So you, out of everyone, should understand the importance of protecting this art. The secrets that we're responsible for, and the sacrifices it takes to keep them out of the wrong hands. I've been working for over a century and still have much to learn."

Razzle listened astutely. "I truly am sorry for my disrespect, sir. There is no excuse. I just want to return to my old self. If I get the chance to be human again, then I would appreciate the opportunity to learn."

Azoria, taking in the conversation, looked at Jandar in shock. "He's human? How'd he learn elven?"

Jandar, focused on the main conversation, whispered, "I taught him. He actually pays attention."

Meanwhile, Darius laughed at the cat's desperate request. "Young Razzle, you're wasting your time. I couldn't reverse your spell even if I wanted to. You see, the spell that binds you is only unbound by the caster. You'd need to defer your apologies to Sir Boltbeard."

Razzle was disheartened, "Oh no... Sir Boltbeard passed away. That means I'm locked in this stupid cat's body for the remainder of my days."

"I'm sorry for *his* loss," Darius said.

A calm voice of a woman broke the conversion. "There is another option." Using telekinesis, a green-skinned lady sitting on a couch summoned her drink from a nearby table. She caught the room's attention and slowly sipped from the floating glass. "The Artificer's Decree, Schema's Notation." She closed her eyes as a thick, hard-covered book in terrible condition rose from a bookshelf and over to Darius. The book flipped toward the middle and presented itself to him. The lady recited aloud from memory. "Section IV: An apprentice can reclaim their status among another magus by acquiring victory from a like-apprentice. Student law applies."

"Interesting." Darius was astonished. "I almost forgot about this."

"Come on, Darius. Give the cat a chance," the green-skinned lady said. "Besides, seeing what your apprentice has learned over the years might be fun."

Others chimed in. "Here, here! Besides, we haven't had some fun around here in a while!"

"Fair enough," said Darius. "Against my better judgment, and in the name of sheer boredom, I declare the challenge approved." His beard raised the quill into the air with excitement. The room broke out in cheers.

Azoria and Jandar were relieved, but Razzle gave no appreciation. He had an idea of what would come and what Darius might say.

"This challenge will be regulated by application of the student law!" Darius said. The room continued in applause and cheers. Several mages walked over to Darius' apprentice to congratulate and encourage her.

Azoria, confused, asked, "Wait, what's student law?"

Razzle turned to the duo. "Student law allows dueling apprentices to use a student ring. It's the final test before an apprentice graduates to a mage!"

"That's great!" Jandar exclaimed. "So that means if you win, you can graduate?"

"Certainly not," Darius roared above the crowd, surprising the new guests with his selective hearing. "Not for Razzle. I will reverse the spell. He must win for the spell to become permanent. Then he's bound by me as my apprentice until he achieves mage status. In the meantime, if my current apprentice wins, she'll graduate to the mage level, and Razzle will return to cat form."

"That's still good, right?" Jandar asked.

"Kind of, but not really," Razzle said. "He's agreed to temporarily turn me back to human form so I can participate in this challenge. They call it *Ring Roulette*. We each get a student ring to wear on our finger. These rings contain random spells in ancient text. The words of the spells project from our rings. The goal is to identify and use the correct spells. If we mispronounce or cast an incorrect spell, we lose a point and even injure ourselves!"

"Okay…" Azoria was confused. "And so you…"

Razzle was panicking. "I never studied long enough to know how to wield the ring! I probably recognize less than half of the spells. I have no idea what most of those spells do. Some spells can affect her, and others can affect me!"

"Interesting," Jandar said. "That lady-mage over there didn't do this to give you a chance, Razzle." The green-skinned lady nodded toward Jandar and his group with a mischievous smile. He kept his eyes fixed on her. "She did it to help the other apprentice."

Darius called on Razzle to step forward. "May this be your last steps as a feline."

Razzle stepped forward. "Here we go."

"Wait," Jandar said. "Razzle, you don't have to do this."

"Actually, I do," said Razzle. "I'm paranoid of hawks! I'm tired of looking overhead for flying predators when I poop outside! I'm sick of randomly purring and pressing my face against everything I see!" Razzle paced back and forth. "My stomach hurts from constantly coughing up hairballs."

"You? I'm stuck cleaning it up," Jandar said.

Razzle raced back to Jandar and leaped in his arms. Filled with sarcasm, he placed his tiny furry paw over Jandar's lips. "Shhh, save your words, dear sir. By the way, I cover my litter with this paw."

Azoria bellowed with laughter as Jandar tossed him back to the ground. "Where's a hawk when you need one?"

As the others chuckled at the impromptu exchange, Razzle sprung toward Darius. Near Razzle was another cat lying on the floor. The slender black cat was asleep and nestled into itself. It uncoiled as it noticed Razzle dropping down near it.

"And what did you do to deserve this?" Razzle asked.

"Uh, no… That's just a regular ol' cat," Darius' apprentice said.

Sir Darius prepared the incantation as the black cat popped up and scurried away. He lit a candle on his desk that radiated a blue light. Then Darius picked up a silver staff and tapped it against the candle holder. Each tap gave Razzle an explosive spark as he recited the spell, slightly shocking him. Razzle screamed in unexpected agony. Jandar caught himself reaching for his knife, an instinctive response to seeing Razzle in pain.

The green lady's soothing voice said, "This spell was meant to be painful to break. This is part of his penance."

Azoria gasped as she watched the little cat scurry as loud popping sounds shot Razzle off his feet. Darius' voice grew louder and bolstered across the room's walls. Razzle continued to scream, but it was more out of fear than pain. As Darius ended the incantation, the light from the candle spread across his desk and onto Razzle. The blue light brightened the entire room as it covered Razzle's outline. Then, his shape morphed from a cat and into a young human. As the light dispersed, Razzle realized he was on two feet and looking at his hands. His old garbs were still on him, albeit rather tight. He laughed as the crowd cheered.

"Wow! You did it, Sir Darius!" Razzle said. "I can't believe this! I can walk! Look at me!"

The smiles were temporary as Darius' message darkened the mood. "Razzle, your ring." He passed him a silver ring with a red ruby in the middle. "The other apprentice already had hers on. At the fifth dusk, when the moon settles above the Traveler's Star, we shall meet at the city's southern entrance. You both have limited charges, so as long as you're outside of the city walls, you can practice a bit. As you know, these are real spells and can be dangerous when cast!"

The excitement wore off. Razzle was returning to reality. He comprehended the gravity of the situation. Disheartened, he turned to walk out of the building's traditional exit as the crowd thinned out. Azoria, on the other hand, was intrigued. She approached Razzle with her hand out, slowly touching his face. "You're human," she said in amazement. She felt the contour of his cheekbones, giggling at his lack of fur and whiskers.

Razzle awkwardly froze in confusion. "Did I forget to tell you I'm human?" he asked. He was a bit taller than her, with scrawny limbs and wavy bunches of brown hair flowing past his ears. He combed his bangs back through his fingers.

A normal person might find her curiosity a bit awkward, but Razzle barely paid attention. He was so preoccupied with worry that he stumbled into a chair on the way out of the building.

"Come on, Razzle," Azoria said. "You're being too hard on yourself! I say we go practice for a spell. Get it?" She laughed, somewhat impressed with her sense of humor.

"What's the use?" asked Razzle. "I was a terrible cat! I'm a worse human. There's just not enough time to figure out this damn ring."

Jandar, searching for answers, said, "It's obvious they want you to lose. Maybe the answer isn't outside the city walls. Maybe it's back in that room."

"What do you mean?" asked Azoria.

"Well, there may be books in there that Razzle could look through before the test.

"That's an option," Razzle sarcastically responded. "I'm sure I can concentrate enough to study right after morphing into a human, especially with all this stress."

Jandar smiled. "Kid, this isn't stress. There's lots more disappointment to look forward to."

"Oh, that's encouraging! Now I'm really in the studying mood!"

"Well, it beats complaining about it," Azoria said.

"Listen, you don't understand. If I win, I'm his prisoner—apprentice. If I fail, he turns me back into a damn cat, whiskers and all. So, even if I win, I lose!"

While Azoria and Razzle bickered, Jandar couldn't help but notice the eye contact shooting back at him from the tall, elegantly dressed green-skinned mage. He exhaled slowly and stepped past the two squabbling tweens.

"Wait here. I'll be right back," Jandar said. He made his way over to the green-toned lady. She noticed him coming. She was taller than him, with her long neck and slender body. She wore a black gown with a wide collar and gold trimmings that matched her hooped earrings. As Jandar came forward, she waved her apprentice away.

"Well, I couldn't imagine you'd show your face around Ceres-bow after what happened last time," she said.

"Thank you, Nashara," Jandar gratefully replied. "What you're doing for Razzle is appreciated."

"This was more for me." Nashara giggled. "Darius and I have a friendly rivalry. Anything I can do to frustrate him amuses me."

Jandar agreed, unwittingly presenting his charming grin. "And that's why I'm here. We both need something. I'm hoping we can help each other."

"Oh, Jandar. You sure are full of surprises. Well, maybe for some. But not to me. *Sensores* have that ability."

"Exactly."

"You're here because of the girl. That's Azoria?"

"Yes."

"So, the time has come. She already possesses the Klarion. I sensed the magic."

"Yeah. It's a long story."

"If I saw it, then others have too. Would you like me to speak with her?"

"I do. That's what Janella would want."

Nashara waved her hand. "I remember what she asked. Bring her here."

Jandar turned back to motion Azoria over, but she was gone.

CHAPTER

Eight

FRIENDS UNFORESEEN

Azoria hurried after Razzle, who had erratically run from the hall in despair. He was breathing heavily and cursing at himself when Azoria caught up to him. Azoria breathed deeply. She didn't want to irritate Razzle, but there must have been some way for her to help build some confidence in him. "Razzle, over two season ago, I lost everyone I'd ever known. Before I met you and Jandar, I didn't think I could go on. My whole life was torn apart, and I had to figure out what to do next. But now I feel a sense of purpose. We'll still be here for you no matter what happens."

Razzle sneered. "Thanks, but you do know that cats only live for about 15 years, right?"

Dumfounded, Azoria felt a sense of urgency sweep through her. "Acha! We need to find a way for you to get out of this mess."

As she finished her sentence, she spotted a group of red-skinned orcs hastily crossing the street. She l While she had never seen desert orcs, she figured they were just as malicious as the green ones she'd encountered. Razzle saw them too, then turned to Azoria for affirmation.

"I see them," she said.

The orcs were too far ahead to notice her. Two orcs were carrying a large wooden post at both ends, with an iron cage hanging from the middle. There was a figure in the cage, but she couldn't determine what it was. She threw her hoodie over her head and raised her scarf over the lower half of her face like a makeshift mask. Only her eyes were visible.

"This isn't a good idea," Razzle said. "Besides, you have no idea who's in the cage. Maybe they deserve it?"

"I can't believe this town allows orcs to walk freely. They shouldn't be allowed anywhere around here."

"There are thousands of orcs and countless tribes scattered around these parts. We can't fight every orc."

"I don't need to fight every orc, Razzle. I just need to find the ones who killed my dad."

"Okay, but don't you think covering your face makes you look more suspicious?"

There was no response. Azoria sped up, jogging well behind the orcs, lightly hunched over and scurrying around objects and pedestrians. The orcs were headed toward the stables. Overcome with a feeling that he was being followed, one of the orcs looked back in Azoria's direction. Azoria immediately bent down as if tying her boot. Razzle froze, then copied Azoria. The attempt at being discreet looked more like a comedic folly of sorts.

Azoria kept her head down, studying her boot. "Really? There wasn't anything else you could have done?" she violently whispered, clearly irritated. "I think I preferred you as a cat!"

However, the orcs hardly seemed fazed as they continued their way to the stables at the end of the road. Before the stables sat a half-demolished, abandoned building made of stone and mud. The duo made a beeline for one of the stone walls and sat against it.

"What are we doing, Azoria? I mean, we could have just walked by, and they wouldn't have cared.

"Shhh!"

"I have to study!"

"Oh, so now you wanna study?"

The orcs had somebody in the iron cage that hung from the post. Whoever was in there was unconscious and emaciated. Azoria could see that the figure's ears were shaped like hers—an elf's. Her skin turned hot, and her heart beat like a war drum. She reached behind her back for her blade handle.

"No. No, no, no! Calm down, Zorie. This isn't right," Razzle declared.

Azoria looked back at Razzle, tears running down her face. "Leave, then. You wouldn't understand. You're human!"

"Wait just a second." Razzle realized just how serious the situation was becoming. He had enough to worry about, and this moment may shift the entire course of the evening for the worse.

"Do you not remember the last time you faced off against orcs? You barely made it out with your life."

"It's different now, Razzle. I can handle myself." Her voice suddenly lowered a few octaves. "I'm not walking away from this." Her words were spoken with a confidence that Razzle surely knew there was no sense in debating.

Azoria rose, head just barely poking over the corner of the wall. She continued to slowly pull her blade from behind her back. There was no plan except to charge, attack, and free the person in the cage. Whatever happens, happens.

Razzle muttered to himself. "Why are we trying to help someone we don't even know? I'm not getting killed for anybody."

"Shhh!" Azoria shushed him, focusing on the orcs a few dozen yards before them.

As she stepped from behind the wall to begin her charge, a strong arm grabbed her shoulder and pulled her back. She tried to pull the remaining blade portion out, but the hand spun her around too quickly.

"Stop." It was Jandar. "What do you think you're doing?" Azoria's shock at seeing Jandar temporarily diverted her anger. "Think it through, Azoria. Let's fall back and discuss this. Looks like they're settling in. We have time."

Azoria slid the blade back into the sheath, eyes intent on Jandar. "Maybe that elf doesn't."

"I understand. Let's figure something out."

A deep voice roared from the other side of the wall. The footsteps crunching the grass gave clear notice an orc was stepping closer.

"Oi! We gotta problem here?" the orc said.

Unsure what to do, Razzle bent down to 'tie his bootstrings.' Jandar walked around the wall to meet the orc. "No, sir. We were just admiring your tooth necklace. Are those sabretooths? The kids were just checking them out. You know children—always curious!" he said, trying to defuse the situation.

"I suggest you scoot outta here and stop wasting our time!" the taller, pudgier of the orcs yelled.

"I certainly will." Jandar looked back behind the wall. Azoria and Razzle were gone again. As he peered over an orc's left shoulder, he saw two figures approximately twenty yards away rushing to the stable cage.

"I noticed you're riding those large stomptrotters," Jandar said loudly, stalling. "I've been told they're just giant horses with horns. Is that true?"

Azoria and Razzle heard Jandar buying them time as they made their way to the cage. The elf was lying on his side, back to the rescuers. Azoria wasted no time attempting to get a look at him. Then she glanced over at Razzle. "You have anything that can break the lock?"

"Shouldn't we have figured that out before we ran up here? I mean, these things work out better when there's some planning and preparation."

Azoria was not amused. "Hurry! Do you have something or not?"

"Umm, I haven't worn clothes in a long time. Maybe I have something. Lemme check my pockets."

They both vigorously patted their clothes as if they were being attacked by red ants.

"I have nothing. Wait—found something." Razzle pulled an old key on a thin metal ring

from one of his pockets.

"Gimme," Azoria said.

"I'm just guessing, but I'm pretty sure *that* key won't work on *that* lock," Razzle said in a panic.

"It's the ring I want." Azoria pushed her knife between the layers of the keyring and pulled it into the shape of a distressed spiral. She took one end and used it to play with the iron lock.

"You're taking too long," said Razzle.

"Shut up, I almost have it," Azoria said. "Jandar showed me this, but it's been a while. I just have to feel for the dangly piece."

As they bent over the cage lock with Razzle coaching Azoria with words of discouragement like, "There's not enough time," and "You can't do it, give up," the lock popped open.

Azoria leered at Razzle. "Thanks for the positivity."

They opened the cage door, but not without some loud shrilling noise from the hinges. Fortunately, the orcs crowded around Jandar did not hear the high-pitched screeches. Unfortunately, the orcs they hadn't seen behind the stable did. Azoria rushed into the cage and placed the elf on his back. She began dragging the elf backward out of the cage. The elven boy's hair was so long it covered his face. She couldn't get a good look at him. Azoria quickly realized that an unconscious body was heavier than she'd imagined. It took all the strength in her lower body to pull him out. Her quads were on fire, causing her to fall back several times. However, she was able to pull him out merely a few feet from the cage. She believed this would take a lot longer than she imagined.

"Here, I can take over," said Razzle.

"No, I can do it."

"Typical Zorie, just as hardheaded and stubborn as always."

"Just keep watch on the orcs."

"If we can wake him up, maybe we can all run outta here."

She couldn't see the person's face, but that didn't matter. She was helping her kind from whatever horrible atrocities these orcs may have done to him. Razzle, with a deluged sense of urgency, struggled to help pick the elf up. He was still weak from the spell.

"Wow, I had no idea how many uses there were for horse dung!" Jandar shouted, an ill attempt at maintaining the orc's attention.

Azoria and Razzle each took an arm of the elf and slung them over their shoulders. The elf's feet dragged through the dirt and mud as they made their way opposite Jandar. They desperately searched for an exit around the end of the stable wall. As they turned a corner, another orc appeared.

"Well, well, looky-looky!" A menacing orc towered over them, horsewhip in hand. His amber skin was characteristic of the desert orcs. Razzle had never come this close to an orc before. He first noticed the rancid body odor that attacked all his senses simultaneously. Razzle was just about eye level with his abdomen, which was as wide as two of him. Animal skulls protected the orc's shoulders and leather necklaces covered his upper chest. His biceps were the shape of giant eggs, with thick veins protruding down the front. His forearms were built like they could block a direct blow from an experienced swordsman.

Azoria never looked up. The half-year preparing for fighting meant nothing at that moment. All her vengeful rage escaped her. All the memories flooded back into her mind; their power, their bloodlust. She heard that an orc's threshold for pain was far higher than most other beings. To Azoria, the orc was more than a being. It represented the devastation of her life, the loss of her loved ones, and the end of a world she longed to be a part of again. Its pig-like nose, elongated forehead and wide eyes. His fanged teeth were just long enough to be seen through closed lips. In all the times Azoria had imagined this confrontation—the preparation and training, the memories and hatred within her—this couldn't have gone any more opposite. There she stood, small and vulnerable.

Razzle whispered to Azoria. "Do something!"

But Azoria couldn't. She dared not to make eye contact with the beast before them. The orc took the black leather horsewhip and thrashed it against Azoria's chest. She fell back, bringing the elf down with her. Razzle, who was usually the jovial of the bunch, screamed out to the orc. "Don't touch her!" He ran forward again and swung his fist against the orc's midsection, doing little more than catch his attention. The orc threw his left arm out and backhanded Razzle. Jandar, still with the other orcs, couldn't see the quarrel from his point of view.

"Dumb kids. I should kill you for trying to steal my bounty. Or maybe I'll just take you with me instead!"

Razzle fell back but quickly regained his footing. As the orc advanced toward the elf, Razzle searched for a solution. He was obviously not strong enough to engage in fisticuffs, and there was nothing around him he would consider a weapon. Then he remembered the student ring on his left hand. He waved his right hand over the right to activate it. A large projection of words shot out of the ring, approximately one foot in front of Razzle's face.

The orc noticed the red-lighted banner projected from Razzle's ring. "Oi! We got us a magic user," the orc grunted.

There was no going back. Whatever spell Razzle released would have consequences. The spell that hovered over his hand was in common lettering, but he couldn't understand it. Razzle took a few steps back to give space between him and the oncoming orc. "Kawani… manto…kari!" Razzle yelled. He squeezed his eyes shut in anticipation of some sort of bright light or explosion, but there was none. Instead, a projectile shot from his hand. Opening his eyes, he saw a live chicken in mid-air, flapping its wings toward the orc. The menacing face of the orc changed to confusion. The chicken tried to maintain its lift. Its feathers sprawling and sporadic clucking brought the orc to unexpected laughter. Not sure what to do next, Razzle chimed in on the laughter, eyes wearily staring at the orc.

"That was hilarious, my boy! You are too funny to kill! Yes, I will keep you for myself!" the orc said. Razzle's laughter subsided as he quickly swiped over the ring to the next spell.

The next one was a language he had never seen. He had no idea how to pronounce the lines and dots that were formed in front of him. Then, he noticed something moving behind the orc. It was Azoria. "Step away from him."

The orc slowly turned around to see what kind of paltry challenger approached from behind him. To his surprise, Azoria gripped both hands around the Klarion in a high guard. "That's a cute toy there, elf." As the words left his mouth, the flash of the Klarion whizzed near his face. He looked down only to see his horsewhip in two pieces. As the top half fell to the ground, the orc said, "Alright there, little one. You're starting to piss me off a bit."

Jandar had exhausted the conversation with the trio of orcs when something across the stable caught their attention. He watched Razzle fall and then a red light shined in from his ring. Then he saw an orc marching at him. The orc trio saw it too, and turned to run toward the action. Jandar slid behind and tripped one of the orcs. He slowed one down a tick, but Jandar knew taking on three would be dangerous. Desert orcs weren't as strong as their high-forest breth¬ren, but they were extremely quick and their skin was callous due to their many years under the sun. As Jandar moved to drop-kick the next orc in his back, he was in full view of the melee.

There was Azoria, half the size of this orc, with the Klarion displayed.

"Azoria, no!" Jandar commanded. "Put it away!"

For Azoria, there was no going back. Even with all that Jandar had taught her, she was not strong enough to fight the orc without the Klarion. The flashbacks of the unimaginable beatings she had endured from the creatures and knowing what may have just happened to Razzle. She didn't care what could take place after this particular skirmish. She wasn't mature enough to control her emotions or to think what troubles may lay waiting for them after she killed them. She did not comprehend city politics, who these orcs may be connected to, or their mission.

"Azoria, is that you?" A familiar voice rose from the ground next to her. The voice rang like a klaxon, forcing her to briefly take her eyes off the shocked orc. The elf on the ground woke up. His long, brown hair that was once hung over his face was now lying to the side. Through the bruising around his eyes, the swollen cheek, and the scruffy facial hair, Azoria immediately recognized him.

"Gymmal?"

She looked forward again and could see Jandar tussling with the three orcs, which he had managed to slow down as they'd come up the field. The orc in front of her dropped the handle portion of his horsewhip and pulled out his wooden club. Razzle was still flipping through his spells as Gymmal was attempting to pick himself off the dirt.

"And what exactly are you gonna do with that, little girl? Kill me?" the orc said as he swung his club out toward Azoria.

"If you're lucky, it'll be quick," she said.

A brick hovered and dropped between them as they moved toward each other. As quickly as they'd seen the first one, dozens more circled them. "Razzle, are you doing this?" Azoria yelled, eyes still focused on her adversary.

"No, not me," Razzle called back in awe. Dozens of bricks turned to hundreds as more piled up between Azoria and the orc. By the time Razzle responded, a storm of stones had formed into a wall. All the stone and other building materials were somehow rising from the various piles of old walls and transforming around the orc. Azoria could no longer see her rival.

Two horses appeared on her side of the wall, with Nashara at the lead. "Hurry, let's go!" She offered with her hand out. The welcomed relief couldn't have come at a greater time. Azoria quickly helped push Gymmal onto the horse and lifted herself up after. Jandar made it on top of the stable rooftop and over the other side. He jumped onto the other horse and helped pull Razzle up. The stone-imprisoned orc angrily smashed his way out. The others caught up with him in pursuit of their stolen horses. They attempted a futile run to catch up to the evaders, but the inept rescuers quickly galloped off.

Outside of Ceresbow, furlongs of neighborhoods sprawled to the east. They raced toward an old abandoned church with long cellar doors made of iron protruding from the ground. Nashara sent the horses off toward town through the east, and the group made their way underground. They followed Nashara through a maze of hallways that led even further down. Eventually, they made their way into a large den area well-lit and decorated with exotic objects. Azoria was quiet, eager to enter the den just to speak to Gymmal. As soon as they entered, Azoria turned and hugged Gymmal. Tears ran down her face as she quietly held him. Gymmal, too weak to keep his arms up, lightly patted her back.

"Gymmal, what happened to you?"

Before Gymmal could speak, a thunderous voice shot out from behind him.

"You almost got us arrested, Azoria! Or worse yet—killed!" Jandar was uncharacteristically furious. Azoria's trance of comfort was shattered by his voice. "What were you thinking? After all our time together! The training and the work, and you figured *now* would be a good idea to show off the Klarion?" Jandar yelled.

Azoria, with her mouth wide open, displayed her clear expression of shock. She felt blindsided by his frustration.

"For as much as Jandar and I have our differences, I fully agree with him. That was very foolish," Nashara added.

"I… I just saved someone's life. Turned out to be my best friend! I didn't think he had survived the raid in our village. I was able to—"

"Almost get us killed!" Jandar said. "Imagine if you had murdered that orc. Then where would we be? They hang criminals for less around here. Plus, with Nashara helping, you could have gotten her killed! That's another motherless child."

Azoria's face turned somber. Nashara pivoted to Jandar. "Sir Jandar, might you entertain me in conversation?" She walked toward the corner of the room with Jandar closely behind.

"By withholding information from her, you're doing more harm than good. You're holding her back from her destiny. And the longer it takes, the stronger her enemies get—*our* enemies. The more you fight her, the more she'll pull away."

"Oh, she pulled away, alright! Running down the street like a lunatic."

"I'm sure she learned from this experience. She'll be better next time."

"There won't be a next time. This little experiment is done."

"That's not for you to say."

"Nashara, you didn't see what happened to her. You didn't have to take care of her after being beaten to her last breath. Death standing at her bedside. I had to look after her every day, wondering if she'd ever wake up."

"I could never imagine what you had to endure, especially after losing your family. But she survived. Her recovery might be proof that she is, in fact, ready for this."

"She needs to be protected."

"But *she* is the protector."

"*She* is just a kid!"

"Really? Azoria's almost the same age as the boys in her village when they begin their warrior trials. There's practically no difference when it comes to age. You can't undo the last half-year of her life. She's here with all the pain, experience, and training. She'll never go back to toys and games. Azoria is no longer the little girl her father knew, but she's the fighter her father would be proud of."

Azoria couldn't make out what they were discussing. She was fixated on Gymmal. She turned and hugged him with all her might. Gymmal returned the gesture and wrapped his hands around her.

"This is surreal. I can't believe you're here!" Azoria said.

"It wasn't easy, Zorie. We should have gone with you. I led everyone to danger. We didn't even make it back to the forest. I'm always failing," Gymmal said in disappointment.

Azoria pushed him away to get a good look at him. She shook him by his shoulders, as if trying to wake him from self-pity. "It took a lot of bravery to escape. You know where they're at! I say we go get them."

"Young lady." Nashara bent down and took Azoria's hand. In contrast to Jandar, her face was kind, and her voice was soft. "I witnessed what happened. I was there through most of it. You are courageous for rushing in to help free your friend. But next time, seek help first. Perhaps Jandar could have made a plan that may have saved your friend without causing a scene."

After tending to Gymmal's wounds, Nashara brought Azoria to a separate room. "Do you know what I am?" she asked.

Azoria shrugged. "This is the farthest I've traveled from Averstone. I've only seen elves, humans, and…orcs."

Nashara beamed. "Yes, this has been a huge day for you. I could only imagine the excitement you've had." She placed her hand over her own heart. "I am a Sensore. Even if you knew what I was, meeting us is very rare. There's few of us left in this world."

Azoria stared blankly at her.

"Sensores possess a unique ability. As you know, we can move things with our minds. Some of us can even communicate through our minds."

Azoria suddenly realized that Nashara wasn't moving her mouth. Her voice was in her head. Stunned, Azoria shot out of her seat, searching the room for an answer.

130

Nashara giggled and gently waved her back to the chair. "I'm sorry; next time, I will use my mouth to speak."

Azoria awkwardly slid back into her seat. Nashara continued. "Sensores can sense in different ways than common beings. We're gifted with the ability to receive visions of important events from the past, present, and future."

"You can see the future?" Azoria asked.

"Not quite. We can see bits of the events and try to interpret them. Long ago, there were many of us. We used to aid kings and generals. Then, we became the targets of the Asharyins during the Great Disorder. Some aligned with the enemy to stop us from providing important information against their adversaries. It was an age when the heavens and the hells played the kingdoms of the Earth against one another."

"Wow… That's a lot."

"There's more I need to tell you," Nashara said. "There's a lot I know about you. And we are connected in many ways. First, let's get this out of the way. Jandar is indeed your uncle. I've known Jandar and your mother, Janella for their entire lives."

A tear fell from Azoria's eyes.

Nashara continued. "I understand that Jandar gave you Janella's letter. Allow me to help you understand." Nashara swirled her hands until a projection of images appeared. "Azoria, your ancestors were riders of the Klarion Dragons—holy dragons who were once sent from the

Celestial realms to protect Galvardia."

Azoria gulped aloud, her eyes wide and intense as she stared at the images of giant dragons that resembled blue crystal, flying the skies above grand cities. Azoria was astonished by Nashara's visuals as she narrated. "Asharyin demons invaded the Celestial realm and war ensued. A Celestial warrior escaped to Earth. Soon, he met an elven woman, and they fell in love. That woman was your great grandmother, D'Asora."

Nashara continued as Azoria studies the visuals. "They bonded in marriage and D'Asora bore a child. But they could not hide for long. The Asharyins entered our world through the same portal and killed the Celestial. D'Asora was sick with vengeance and brought his blood to the leader of the dragons. Before the Asharyins killed off the Klarion Dragons, the last one sacrificed himself to united his most powerful scale with both the Celestrial's blood and a single tear from D'Asora. The dragons death created your Klarion sword. Your great grandmother dedicated the remainder of her years wielding the Klarion Blade to end the Asharyins' reign. D'Asora became the *Asharyin shikari*; the demon hunter. Only those with Celestial blood can brandish the blade. The Klarion was passed down to your grandmother, then your mother, and now you."

Nashara gave her a moment to collect herself and then said, "We can continue this discussion another time. How about we just rest for tonight?"

"No, I'm fine. I promise," Azoria said. "I'd like to know more. I can handle this."

Nashara looked at her, rather surprised. "Well, I must say, that's a response I wasn't expecting. You're a strong warrior, Shikari."

"So, what happens now?" Azoria asked.

"There's more you should know. Draw your Klarion. The blade itself was imbued from the heart scale of the last Klarion Dragon. The handle was forged of the Celestial's alloy. The cross-guard is a rose stem and forged in silver. That rose stem represents the love between D'Asora and the Celestial. The single silver rose thorn activates the sword's the true powers."

"What do you mean? I've seen the blade lights up. It's like it's speaking to me. You mean to tell me I haven't even activated the sword yet?" Azoria asked.

"No. Not yet. As you know, the blade turns brighter when there is danger or evil lurking about. But when demons are around, it'll call out to you. You'll know when it does. To harness the sword's power, you must do two things. First, you must press your finger over the thorn to draw your Celestial blood. Then you must speak the words on the blade."

Azoria looked at the sword to evaluate its details. Its beauty, from pommel to point, went beyond words. So rich in history, every detail spoke a story she'd never known existed. More than just an opulent conversation piece, its merit filled her with a sense of pride she'd never felt before.

"All of those stories I heard growing up, they were about my family? I have Celestial blood? This is unbelievable! So, what happens when I do those things? Do I get powers or something?"

"Yes," Nashara said. "Something like that."

"I can't read the words on the blade."

Nashara said, "Dear, I have been around for many years. I remember your great grandmother. I was here when the Asharyins invaded our world. I'm one of the few who can read the language of the ancients."

"Why didn't my dad tell me about any of this?"

Nashara, her voice calm and soothing, explained. "It seems all the men in your life feel the need to protect you from your eventual responsibilities. But the longer they deny you, the stronger the remaining Asharyins become. The shikari oath is not taken until the sixteenth year of birth. You are still very young. We can't wait years for your development. Much has happened since your mother's death. Much is expected of you now."

Azoria stared at the clear blade, with its beveled symbols carved on the side.

"Azoria, what's about to happen when you speak these words is something I can't explain. It happened to your elven ancestors before you, and now it is your turn to take the blade. Press your thumb over the thorn spike. You will bleed, and your blood will awaken the sword. You will then read the inscription, '*Illuminus shikari.*' What happens next is something I can't prepare you for."

"What does that mean?" Azoria asked.

"It means to light up the power of the demon hunter. You will feel the warmth of Celestial light that will protect you in battle. By activating this power, you swear to hunt the Asharyins of this world and banish them with the blade."

Azoria stood impassively, as if readying herself for the unpredictable.

"Are you ready to take the mantle of your lineage?" Nashara asked, the images in the air dissipating around her.

Azoria nodded, her teeth tightly pressed on her closed lips in concentration. She pressed her thumb over the silver spike, feeling the pain as it opened her skin. Azoria's immediate reaction was to jerk away, but she caught herself and held on tighter to thorn. Then, she spoke the words. "*Illuminus shikari.*"

THERE WAS ENOUGH ALE TO SPLIT BETWEEN JANDAR, RAZZLE AND Gymmal.

"I've heard a lot about you, Gymmal," Jandar said. "You being here means more to her than you know."

Gymmal took a sip with his left hand, as his right hand was bandaged. "For me, too. I never thought I'd see her again. It was destiny to be rescued by you and Azoria. I'm indebted to you with my life."

"That's not necessary. Azoria was the mastermind behind your rescue. While I may have done things a bit differently, it's Azoria who deserves all the appreciation," Jandar said.

"Sounds like Zorie." Gymmal smiled. "I remember one time this teen took something from one of the elfins. Azoria stepped in to stop him. The teen pushed her down. She landed on her bum in a puddle. Mud was everywhere, on her face and in her hair. Lots of people were laughing. She got right up and punched him in his face. It was hilarious! He was holding his nose, bleeding! That's Zorie for you!"

Jandar returned the smile. "Yep, sounds like her. Anyways, how'd you get out?

"I made my escape with a few other elves. Nobody else made it," Gymmal said. "I guess they sent the desert orcs to find me. They're excellent trackers. I believe they were bringing me back. We've been building something for the orcs. I even saw a human there." Then he gave Razzle a look of distrust.

Razzle put his hands out in front of him. "Whoa, I'm not with them. I mean, I was the one who unlocked your cage, after all!"

"He's good, he's with us," Jandar said.

"Pardon, it's just been a difficult time," said Gymmal.

Jandar peered closer at Gymmal. He observed the scars across his arms and the patch of hair missing from the side of his head. The blood soaked through his fresh bandage that wrapped the rest of his head exhibited just one of the many tortures he must have endured. Gymmal couldn't have been more than 15 years of age. "They clipped your ear?" Jandar asked.

"Yes, sir. That was the orc's way of marking us. They cut half of our left ears. The number of ears had to be the number of slaves when we returned from the mines."

"Not that it's better, but couldn't they have just branded you or something?" Razzle said.

"They hate us," Gymmal said. "They figured if we looked less like elves, then they could stand us long enough not to kill us every day."

Razzle's head sagged downward in grief. Jandar was aware of the atrocities the orcs committed, but seeing it firsthand was difficult. He couldn't find the words to express his empathy. All he could do was refill Gymmal's cup. Gymmal raised his cup in appreciation. As he placed it to his lips, a loud bang shot across the room. A light flashed from the room to the hallway. The trio jumped up in reaction. A wind oscillated throughout as the candles roared into a last dying flame until they sputtered out. A low smoke pushed across the floor toward them as a figure turned the corner. It was Nashara.

"Gentlemen," she said, "the Heir of the Celestial bloodline, the Vanguard Hunter of Demons and Wielder of the Sacred Klarion. I present to you, Azoria Dash, the Asharyin Shikari."

Azoria entered and made her way to the head of the table. She was a few inches taller than usual, her profile cocooned in flames of silver and purple hues. They danced almost like a shifting patina. Her eyes matched the silver flames that surrounded her. The Klarion in her hand pulsated a vibrant turquoise, and the bezels were highlighted in matching silver. The light from the flames spun and danced throughout every edge of the room, in lieu of the dying candles. Razzle jumped up in excitement.

Still reeling from his head wound, Gymmal raised his hands over his eyes to filter the spectacle. He squinted to see her as the shifting of the light overwhelmed his vision. Still, he was mesmerized by the sight before him. It was as if she was forged from the brilliance of electrum. Bright, florescent spectrums of colors bannered behind her and skipped against the walls behind her.

Jandar wore obvious frustration on his face. His brows furrowed. "This is wrong, Nashara. This is dangerous. No less than an hour ago, she irresponsibly brandished the Klarion. Now you reward her with more power?"

Nashara smiled. "She's not being rewarded, Jandar. This is her birthright."

Jandar turned his head in dismissal. With a stern look in Azoria's direction, Nashara said, "I agree. She was irresponsible. I expect her to learn from her irresponsibility through the inherited duty of more responsibility."

"She's not ready," Jandar said.

"I also agree. She's not ready. Neither was her mother. Nor her mother before her. No one is truly ready. Just as her ancestors before her, she will learn. But it's your call, Jandar," Nashara said.

"How does it feel? Shifting?" Gymmal inquired with invigorated wonder.

Azoria, catching her breath, placed her hands over her stomach. "It's like a rush of wind. You know when we used to jump off the rocks and into the creek? It's like that! Like falling, but in a good way."

Nashara interrupted. "Azoria has a lot to learn about her newly discovered abilities. The rest of you need to prepare. Averstone wasn't the only village overtaken. They're clearing out the Crosslands."

"Who?" Jandar asked.

"The orcs. But they wouldn't dare do this on their own. There's been talk that the Varosians are looking for a special element to create a powerful weapon and have allied with the orc nation. I've been told the orcs will keep the land they conquer if they bring them the element—ellastrium.

"Ellastrium? The green crystals found in the wildwoods?" Jandar asked.

Nashara nodded. "Yes. If you're going to rescue your friends, you'll need the best armament. You're likely to meet powerful enemies and dark magic."

Gymmal agreed. "Yes, those green crystals, that's what they had us mining for at the quarry. Unfortunately, I know that place well."

"You have to understand," Nashara continued, "orcs are a people of war. They're born and bathed in violence. It's their culture."

"If they're born in violence, then I've been baptized in their blood," Azoria said with a newfound confidence.

Nashara looked at Azoria, as if trying to speak beyond her eyes and into her soul. "You'll need to utilize the strengths that make each one of you great. Do not fight them with brute anger. Understand them and use their weaknesses against them. Work as a team, each contributing your abilities that have gotten you this far."

The conversation continued about their plans for rescuing the elves at the quarry. It was a rather risky proposal. After much resistance, Jandar gave in. Once Azoria was aware of her friend's whereabouts, there was no talking her out of a rescue plan. First, he would take Azoria and Gymmal to Kromotana for weapons and training. Then they would head to the quarry to rescue the elven captives. It was determined that Razzle would stay with Nashara. She offered to help tutor him for his upcoming challenge. Jandar figured Razzle's chicken-conjuring spells would be of no use on this mission.

Jandar certainly couldn't do it all by himself. Looking around him, he saw nothing but children. One was a reckless girl with bad decision-making skills, and a boy who set the mage bar pathetically low. Instead of capable reinforcements, he scoffed at the addition of a battered young man, who needed serious recovery, enlisted in their ranks.

"Gymmal's in bad shape. He'll need to rest," said Jandar.

"We don't have time," Gymmal said. "It'll take a few days to travel back east. I can recover along the way. Besides, I promised them I would come back with help and rescue them as soon as possible!"

"Honestly, you're no good to us, kid," said Jandar. "You would only slow us down."

A quietness came over the group. "No, he's not! He has a lot of talents that can help us," Azoria said.

"Like what?"

"Like…he knows how to get us there. He also knows how to get through the quarry, and what dangers are around there." Jandar traded looks at Nashara as Azoria continued. "Oh, and…he's great with a boomerang!"

The group drew in awkward silence until Jandar chuckled aloud. "Boomerangs? Is he good at juggling too?" Razzle mocked.

"Hey, I'm starving. What's for dinner, chicken?" Gymmal retorted snidely.

"That's enough," asserted Jandar.

Gymmal hung his head. "It's okay, Azoria. Maybe they're right."

"No, wait a moment," Nashara said. "You said he's proficient in the boomerang. The boomerang was originally intended as a deadly weapon before it became a kids' toy. If you can use the boomerangs, you can fight. I have a friend in Kromotana. It's been ages since I've seen him. His name is Kilajen, and he's an armorer. He builds all types of weapons. He should have some fetchblades he can lend you. Those will come in handy for a young warrior."

"Fetchblades?"

"Yes. They're boomerangs with blades at the ends. If you're really good, you can wield two at a time. Kilajen knows more about them."

Jandar, who had looked perplexed just minutes before, suddenly seemed more accepting of the idea.

"I was going to pay Kromotana a visit anyway," she said. "But now I can just give you the scroll I needed to pass to him. Would you be willing to stop there?"

Jandar showed his concurrence with a simple head nod.

"I have no shillings. I can't pay him," Gymmal said.

"Don't worry, young one," Nashara said. "You'll find a way. I believe it. Some advice, however. He's an eccentric. A little ego boosting will go a long way."

LATER THAT EVENING, THEY ATE AND REPLENISHED THEIR SUPPLIES. "Gymmal, I can't believe you're here. Are you alright?"

"Zorie, it's been hell. The orcs torture many of the prisoners. They find it funny."

"What about Myra and Sariah?"

"They haven't touched them. They treat the girls surprisingly well. I think they have worse things in store for them." Gymmal started to choke up. "They were going to leave with me, but they were too scared. I'm so glad they didn't because the five others who came with me died. One was Doravon."

"I'm so sorry about your brother, Gymmal," Azoria said, holding back tears.

"I can't believe it," Gymmal said, almost as if he was in a trance. "They didn't even try to capture them. They just killed them."

Azoria felt his emotions. It was contagious. She began to weep too. "We gotta get the rest out of there. I have nothing to live for. I will give my life to release our people."

"Don't say that, Zorie," Razzle said. "You made it. Gymmal made it. You're here for a reason. Now that you have these cool powers, we can do it. Let's make a pact. Starting today, we don't die. Swear?"

Azoria and Gymmal smirked, trying to hold in the giggles. Their resistance lasted a few seconds, then they burst into laughter. "We swear!"

"Okay, so now that's taken care of, can someone please explain what the heck 'alfies' are?" Razzle asked.

Gymmal smiled. "Alfies! Those are delicious! All I remember is how warm they'd be, with the cinnamon sprinkled on top! They're actually called *alfajores*. They're little circle cookies. Like a little sandwich with caramel in the middle."

"Wow! That sounds amazing!" Razzle said. "Your friend Myra is a hero. She sounds like she's worth fighting for!"

Gymmal chuckled. "Yep. They all are."

Having Gymmal around gave Azoria a sense of nostalgia. For just a bit, she forgot how bad things had been without him. She had hope they would reunite with Myra and Sariah once again. Her hope gave her comfort. It was all she had.

Razzle looked down, reminding himself of his upcoming test. "I'm sorry I can't go. I really want to be there with you to help. I guess I'm of no use right now. But I'll study hard. Next time, I'll be ready."

"I'm sure you will, slacker." Azoria laughed. "Wish us all of the luck the earth and sky can offer. We're gonna need it."

A few hours later, Nashara and Jandar headed back up to the surface from a side tunnel. They kept a look out for any signs of angry desert orcs. The coast was clear.

Jandar couldn't help himself. "Earlier, there was talk of a threat. Something that could change the color of the sky?"

"We don't have details yet, but we believe the Varosians are behind the recent raids in the Crosslands. All under the command of their sorceress queen. Azoria's village is the third one they've raided. Lots of refugees have made their way into Ceresbow."

Confused, Jandar asked, "Wait, those weren't humans that attacked Averstone. Those were orcs."

"That's what the council's trying to figure out. It's unlikely, but there may have been an alliance established between the orcs and the humans."

Jandar was visibly frustrated. "I knew they couldn't maintain the treaty. Sooner or later, they'd come for the Crosslands. So, what are you planning to do?"

"Well, the council ordered scouts to follow the desert orcs and inform us of where they're taking the elf prisoner, but Azoria put a stop to that."

"Damnit. So what now?"

"I'm not sure yet." Nashara placed her hand on Jandar's arm. "Just be careful at the quarry. We're not sure what's out there."

Jandar nodded in concurrence.

"Speaking of Azoria, when are you going to tell her?" Nashara asked.

"I don't know. She learned a lot today. I'll let her rest."

"Of course, but you can't keep putting it off."

Jandar pondered at her words. "I'm not putting it off. There's a right time to explain it to

her, and I can never find it."

"You don't want to hurt her, or confuse her anymore," Nashara said. "I understand that. But she's not your daughter."

"You don't think I know that?" Jandar snapped back in fury, cutting her off.

Nashara's voice turned firm. "She's a shikari, you need to treat her as such. No matter how much you protect someone else's child, you can't bring back your own."

"Listen, I'm doing the best that I can. Seriously, Nashara. We just spent over half-a-year in the wilderness."

Nashara remained quiet for a spell, thinking of how to reframe her advice. A few feet away, a herd of goats were nosily grazing behind short wooden posts. She pet one as it brought its head over the posts. "That's what I'm concerned about. As a shikari, there will be times she'll need to go on her missions alone. Will you be okay without her?"

Jandar stood in the breezy night, the cool air carrying the horses' grunts and neighs as they ate from the trough behind him. "She's still family, Nashara. None of this is easy."

"Change isn't easy. It comes when we don't want it to. But it brings unexpected surprises, like this whole thing bringing you and Azoria together again."

Jandar raised his eyebrow as Nashara excused herself back into the basement through the cellar doors. She was always so positive, even in the toughest of times. He wished to possess her patience. "Easy for you to say," Jandar said. "You get to live hundreds of years."

As he laughed, he sensed a presence. Something didn't feel right. It was too quiet. The night breeze introduced a sense of discomfort. Keeping his head straight, he used his peripheral vision to scan the area. He wasn't alone. It couldn't be the desert orcs because they weren't very stealthy. Orcs didn't have the agility that elves and humans possessed. It had to be a tracker.

Jandar turned the corner back to the bunker, his hand on his knife. A shadowy figure outlined in the moonlight stood in front of him. "Good eve, sir," an unexpected yet familiar voice called.

"Colvin?" Jandar asked, already knowing the answer.

"That'll be me."

Colvin stepped forward into the lantern light that hung overhead. It had been years since Jandar had seen him. He'd almost forgotten about him. There was a history between the two men. Colvin often reminded Jandar of himself, another half-breed who'd made it the hard way. He knew Colvin's story. He was a runaway who'd come to the Crosslands. He'd been accepted by those who weren't accepted themselves. He'd grown up fast among hustlers, killers, and opportunists. He'd learned to survive in the streets and eventually became a bounty hunter and hired hand for guides. For years, he'd worked with Colvin, along with countless others. Too many names to remember, and most he'd never see again. But one fateful day, Jandar had misguided travelers off course and into Red Bend. Known as the most dangerous region of the Crosslands, even the most brutal criminals and rogues would never venture there. Jandar had been on another drinking binge. Colvin warned him not to take the travelers through it. Jandar had been sure the area was safe and would save days of travel. All but Jandar, Colvin, and a few injured travelers had survived when they were ambushed by the tieflings. The travelers were from well-to-do families and had issued rewards for their capture.

"I had the drop on you, old friend. You're getting slow."

"Well, I have only two choices, either get old or don't. Guess I'm on the right side if I'm standing here talking to you," Jandar said.

"There must be a reason you're standing in the dark. I'm sure you're not here to catch up on life."

"Actually, I just happened to be in Ceresbow and figured I'd stop by and say hi."

Randomly seeing Colvin meant he was up to his old ways. Before the incident at DarkEver, they'd been good friends. In fact, Jandar had taught him many skills he'd learned in the military. He'd taken Colvin under his wing, like Azoria. Jandar had confided in him about losing his family. Colvin had been the only person he didn't punch out for confronting him about his heavy drinking. After the incident, they never spoke again. Colvin being here tonight couldn't be anything good.

"What can I help you with, Colvin?"

"It's more like what *I* can help *you* with. There's a little problem I'm having. You see, my employers are looking for a sword. I guess it looks like it's made of glass. Do you know anything about it?"

Jandar gave Colvin a dead-eye stare. "Well, if you're here asking questions, then I'm sure you already have your answer."

Colvin chuckled. "Yeah, I guess I do."

Jandar leaned against the wall while moving his right hand, gripping the handle to the knife on his belt. He sized up Colvin, who was obviously younger and quicker. A small crossbow was strapped around his forearm, although no bolts were chambered. Jandar knew he'd probably take some damage if he rushed Colvin, but there was no way he would allow the young man to get to Azoria.

"Relax, oldie. I'm not here to collect. I want to make an offer."

"Well, that's certainly better than what might have happened."

"Look, we're both opportunists. They're willing to pay me a lot of money for the blade. Now they've also been tracking me, making sure I'm doing my job."

Jandar's eyes searched the building rooftops above for any sign of others. Besides Colvin, the night was dead silent. "I'm listening."

"They're not watching right now. I lost them a few hours ago." Colvin leaned in as Jandar tightened his grip on his knife. "I'm talking a double-cross," he said. "I need help finding out who the employers are. They're obviously worth a lot of money. They paid me half already. I'll split it with you. You watch my tail and tell me who you see."

Jandar scoffed. "You're a fool if you think I'd fall for this, Colvin. I don't know your angle, and I haven't seen you in years. You suddenly show up here asking for something unobtainable and expect me to just agree to it?"

"No, sir, I don't," Colvin quickly said, his voice a tad louder. He took a breath and returned to a whisper. "Look, I don't care about this blade. I'm just giving some friendly advice, that's all. You have a bullseye on your back. If I don't get this sword, they'll just keep sending mercenaries and bounty hunters until they finally have it. Look, I'm being nice. I'm standing here, unarmed." Colvin raised his hands in a show of peace. "Besides, I'm a gentleman. Am I the type to steal from little girls? The others won't be so nice. They'll slaughter your team and just take the blade. I don't know who they are, and that's where you come in."

Jandar smiled. "Look, son, I'm just a lonely guide taking people where they need to go."

"I know better," Colvin said, his demeanor more serious. "I know you, Jandar. You were a mercenary, a ranger. That never leaves your blood. You can't hide from your past. Whether it's me or someone else, it always catches up."

"Why are you telling me this?" Jandar asked. "Why are you suddenly being such a good friend?"

Colvin settled his hands back to his sides. "Look, we've had our problems in the past, but they're not worth killing for. Be happy I took this job. Who knows what would have happened by now if someone else had?"

Jandar wanted no part of it. He was alarmed by the offer. Then again, Colvin had clearly tracked them. Azoria's public missteps had all but gifted Colvin the sword, and yet he hadn't struck. Was he tipping his hand, or was it something more nefarious?

Colvin continued. "I'm thinking we bait them in. With the two of us teaming up, it's the best chance we have at getting the reward and keeping the sword."

Jandar thought that if he agreed, he could at least keep an eye on Colvin. Now that he knew a third party was monitoring them both, he could use Colvin long enough to keep them at bay and rescue the elfins. *One thing at a time*, he thought to himself.

"Alright, Colvin. If your word is truth, then prove it by keeping them off my back for a few days. Tell them you lost track. I have a few things to tend to. I'm headed near the Varosian border. Give me some time, and I'll meet you in Ceresbow in a week. We'll discuss more then."

Colvin extended his arm out to offer a handshake. "We got a deal?"

Jandar placed his hood over his head, ignoring Colvin's hand. "You may recall that I'm not big on shaking hands. But you have a deal. You better take off before anyone finds out."

"Fair enough." Colvin gave a look of frustration but kept his composure. He turned his back and began walking down the road. "I'll be in touch."

THE MORNING BEFORE THE TEAM DEPARTED TO KROMOTANA, RAZZLE surprised them with an unintended pun. He felt guilty about not being able to go with them on their adventure, so he'd woken up early to practice spells with his student ring. Unfortunately, it hadn't gone the way he'd anticipated.

"Where's Razzle?" Jandar asked Nashara as he gave her a thankful hug for her hospitality. He looked back at Azoria and Gymmal, who were already on their stomptrodders. "The kids want to say goodbye."

Nashara grinned. "He should be on his way. He's probably just taking a few to fix a thing or two."

"What'd he do?" Jandar chuckled as he lifted himself onto his stomptrodder.

As Nashara was about to explain, Razzle arrived. Jandar hardly recognized him. From head to toe, his skin was a dull purple color, with large pink polka-dot blotches all over. His once wavy hair now stuck straight up, as if he'd been electrocuted. Behind him clucked three confused chickens and a spry duck.

Azoria was at a loss for words. Gymmal broke out in laughter.

"Why?" Jandar could barely form a single word around his howling guffaw.

"Alright. Go ahead. Get it all out." Razzle spread his hands out and bowed, as if he was the star actor at the end of a grand performance. "I just wanted to go with you guys. I figured I'd be useful if I could get these spells down."

"I appreciate your effort." Jandar continued to laugh. "We'll deal with the bad guys. If I happen to be in need of a farm, however, you'll be first on my list."

"Yeah. Razzle, the wizard-farmer," Gymmal said as he rode off.

Azoria smiled back at him. "I think it's a cool trick. I mean, who else can make food in an instant? A wizard-farmer sounds like the best of both worlds!"

As the party trotted off, he and Nashara smiled and waved.

CHAPTER
Nine

TRUTH LIES IN KROMOTANA

K romotata was a brilliant city. Its' luster shined well before they made it to the gates. Sunlight gleamed across its' futuristic buildings like a beacon for visitors miles away. Everything looked to be constructed of a shiny alloy material. Even the soldiers' uniforms at the entry gate appeared to possess no stitching in their armor. It bent and flowed with their movements as an entirely seamless piece. With their gleaming weapons, the soldiers escorted them to meet Kilajen the Tinkerer.

Kilajen was an older, yet vibrant gentleman. His gray and white hair coiled into a ponytail, his thick, leathery apron matching the caramel color of his skin tone; both aged. Kilajen welcomed them into his forge. The brick walls were lined with weapons of varying shapes and sizes. Broadswords, arrows, war hammers, maces—all

created from different materials. All looked more like eccentric pieces of art and less like weapons, designed with ease and contour in
mind of the wielder. They reflected Kilajen's eccentric persona. The
amber light glowing from the lava-liquid within the iron caldron
flared across the room.

Jandar handed the scroll over as Kilajen removed his thick,
leather mittens. "So, Nashara vouches for you. You must be rather
important," he said, examining the contents.

"I wish we were. Nashara said you were the most experienced
and knowledgeable armorer in the Crosslands."

Kilajen laughed. "Well, that's a helluva compliment, but I tend
to agree with her."

He offered the party tea as they sat at a long rectangular table.
The tea was as warm as the room.

"We're in need of weapons for this young one. Nashara believed
you may have some fetchblades to lend him." Jandar nodded toward
Gymmal.

"Well, I'll have you know that some of my beauties can take a
year to create. The detail, the time and dedication…" Kilajen pointed toward a double-bladed staff on the table. "Even the materials
take time to find. Each piece is like my very own child." He scanned
the guests sitting across from him. "Nashara is better at trusting people, but that's where we differ. I don't know you, and doubt I'd ever
see my fetchblades again. Offer me something as collateral. A trade,
if you will."

Jandar cleared his throat. "Good sir, what you're asking for isn't
unreasonable. In your shoes, I would likely demand even more. It's
not your demand that we protest, it's that we have nothing of value.
I was a ranger at one time, but now I'm just a guide and a tracker.
There's nothing of value we carry with us."

"Well, I'm sorry for your predicament. How about this? Head
back to Ceresbow and find something of use for me over there."

Azoria, short on patience, had heard enough. "That'll take too
long," she said, her voice heightened. "Orcs burned our village down

and killed my father. There's nothing left. Something is happening here in the Crosslands. Soon, you will not have a home!"

Kilajen chuckled. "Elfin, this facility has been here for eons. It will continue to be here. This invasion of orcs you speak of has been in our ears for decades. I'm sorry, but that is neither my battle nor worry."

Azoria winced at a long sword bracketed on the wall behind him. "I know that blade. One of the orcs had a sword like that."

"That might be true, elfin. I've made hundreds of them. I may have sold it to someone, and that person may have fallen at the hands of an orc. Better yet, I may have *sold* it to an orc."

"You go against your own?"

"Oh, elfin. Please understand that I am tethered to no one. I am a war smith who happens to be paid very handsomely for my creations. Just as you come to me, so do all others. I care not which side. They all have the same excuses to wield weapons."

"That's upsetting. My father was a smith too. He crafted items of peace."

"And where is your father now, dear?" Kilajen asked.

The room went silent as Azoria's burned with anger. Kilajen raised his arms and swung his hands around as if directing an orchestra. He hummed a few notes while making stabbing motions. "I find every fighter to be a member of my orchestra. Each one mastering their instrument of death. And when the battle begins, it's like my favorite maestro conducting the most beautiful symphony. A masterpiece of death, flesh torn to bits in a lock between two opposing forces. The thought of it brings shivers to my skin." Then, he stopped, turned and looked at Azoria, who couldn't believe what she'd just heard. "I do not create the musicians. They must train for years to become perfect. I merely provide the instruments for them to play their masterpieces."

"These weapons are killing your own kind."

"My own? Who? Elves?" Kilajen belted out a huge roar of laughter. "Do you think I represent all of us? Do you think we all

stand together? Half of my people would kill me if given the opportunity. The tribes themselves have been at war with each other since
the beginning. They're feral. The only time they united was for the
Great Disorder. Hell, the orcs sometimes treat me better than my
own people."

"Anyone would be nice to someone who gives them weapons to
kill their enemies."

Jandar interjected. "Azoria, that's enough."

"No, it's okay." Kilajen laughed. "She's right. And I'm fine with
it. Your friend here is mixed," Kilajen said, referring to Jandar. "Why
don't you ask him how the purebloods treated him throughout his
life? I bet that wasn't easy. They couldn't care less, just as long as they
can find someone to be angry with, someone they can look down
upon. If you believe there aren't elven tribes who have committed
great crimes against their own, then you have much to learn."

Kilajen continued. "You, out of all people, have no right to speak
of weapons. You have inherited the most perfect of my family's creations, the Klarion, which fights for what it deems to be good against
evil. It decides. Not you or I. Not the humans, the smallest dwarves,
the biggest giants, nor any ruler. It decides." Kilajen looked at Azoria with disgust. "And you follow its bidding like a slave. You can
tell yourself whatever you want. But you're still just a killer, young
Elfin."

"I've never killed anyone," Azoria said.

"Oh, but you will." Kilajen smirked.

Azoria was clearly upset. Worst yet, humiliated. *How dare he speak
to me like that!* She thought. Under the anger, however, there was humility. The same humility that came after the hag's hut. She realized
that some of Kilajen's words may hold merit. Who defines right and
wrong when everyone has a purpose for their decisions? It conflicted
with her traditional values. She'd never dealt with this lack of moral-
ity growing up. Then again, she'd grown up in a place without these
kinds of politics. Elfins weren't concerned with these things.

"Now I say again, go out and find me something worthwhile. Come back when you have something good to barter with," Kilajen said.

"Wait!" Gymmal shouted. "You're looking for materials for your weapons. I might have something." From under the waistband of his pants, he pulled a small green shard and slid it across the table and into Kilajen's hands.

"Hmmm, is this what I think it is?" he asked.

"Ellastrium, yes," Gymmal said with confidence.

"Interesting. Now you're speaking to me." Kilajen held it in his hand, with wonder in his eyes as if he had just discovered treasure. "Ellastrium can be used to harness and deflect lightning. Enough of it can make some powerful stuff." He took a small golden tube with glass to his eye and inspected the shard.

"You have more of this?"

"That's where we're going. I can bring you more. You loan me the fetchblades and I'll bring more."

"Youngling, if you bring me more, you can keep the fetch-blades." Kilajen rose from the table and walked toward a stack of shelves near the forge. He grabbed two metallic items and handed them to Gymmal. "Funny, I've never gotten a request for these. Usually, I make heavy weapons, but these are fun. Be careful with these; when you push the middle button with your thumbs, they activate the blades at the tip. They work like boomerangs. When they return, the gears inside reverse and deactivate the blades. You'll have to re-activate when you catch them again."

Gymmal held them in his hands. He was still frail. Even if he recovered all his strength, he must train aggressively to master them. They weren't cumbersome, but they were enough to require effort to give it some lift when he threw them.

"Don't worry, Gymmal," Jandar said, noticing the difficulty of holding them. "You'll need some time, but you'll get there."

Gymmal ran his fingers over the edges, drawn to the blinding sheen of light reflecting from its shiny exterior. There were two wings, each with a slot for long blades to protrude like fingernails. He pressed the button in the center, and the blades recoiled. A nervous feeling fell over him; he realized just how real this weapon was and how difficult it might be in practicality. But they were beautiful, and the butterflies in his stomach were equally matched with excitement.

There was an archery field behind the armory where Kilajen took his inventions for testing. It was the perfect area for Gymmal to try out his new gifts. First, he practiced tossing the fetchers and catching them when they returned. He dared not to release the blades. It was all about timing and technique. The soldiers helped teach him simple defense techniques with the fetchers for hand-to-hand combat. They explained to Gymmal that the more he trained, the quicker his muscle memory would respond. Gymmal was quite good for his lack of experience. He was taller for his age, and his thin build allowed him to be more limber. This complemented his quickness.

The soldiers replaced their swords with wooden staffs, which he learned to fight against with his fetchblades. He would cross them above his head, catching the downward swing of the staff. Because the blades arched like cat claws when they protruded, he would activate the blades and slice off that portion of the staff. The blades were also strong enough to damage most standard-issue swords. He quickly learned how to defend with the fetchblade in his left hand, using it as a shield and counter with the one in his right.

The team stayed at Kromotana for three days, dedicating most of their time to training. It was not enough for Gymmal to master any of his new skills, but he was familiar with the basics. His aim and timing were far better with the fetchers than when he'd started. He could aim them at the training dummies and hit their center masses. The training in Kromotana didn't just benefit Gymmal, however. It granted Azoria time to learn more about the Klarion. She had shifted several times by then. The metallic taste in her mouth wasn't as strong, and her recovery became shorter between the transitions. Her left hand, however, was very sore. The continuous puncture wounds to her thumb made it difficult to touch anything with it. Yet, it was a small price to pay for the gift.

The sky was clear, and the sun shone warmly upon them as they left Kromotana. Further east, they headed off on their stomptrotters. Gymmal was riding confidently. Along with the fetchblades, Kilajen had gifted him leather bracers that covered his entire forearms, housing the fetchblades. Azoria rode with a sense of confidence as well. She'd learned a lot about the Klarion Blade. She thought back to what he'd told her. "The Klarion is a wee temperamental. The blade was constructed to take down the Asharyins. Deviate from that, and you'll find its response unpleasant. It's been said that blade wielders who go against the oath of the Klarion will unleash the demons it contains. Don't betray the blade."

THE RIDE TO THE QUARRY WAS QUIET. AZORIA, GYMMAL, AND JANDAR rode under the cloak of night. The moon was full and appeared close enough to touch. Zuna met them at an open passage and scampered to their side. Jandar watched Azoria's demeanor change into serious focus. She was well-aware that the ride meant cutting through what was left of Averstone. It was the quickest way.

Over half a year had passed since the raid, yet the smell of char and ash remained in the air. It brought Azoria to her past. Everything looked different. At the same time, it felt painfully familiar. As they moved closer, Azoria remembered all the residents, reciting where each lived and worked. The skeletons of the old homes barely stood. Her heart sank, and she swallowed the screams she wanted to release down into her guts. Her hands trembled on the stomptrotter's reins. Azoria had never taken the time to deal with her grief and swore she wouldn't start now.

There was little left of the village. The stomptrotters marched through what remained of the main road, stinging the traveler's emotions in savage mockery. Black timber stilts protruded from both sides of the road like silhouettes of headstones in a graveyard. The sound of loons called in the air, giving Gymmal the chills. Jandar rode behind them, watching Gymmal's head swinging from side to side in disbelief. The further they went, the deeper their hearts sank. Gymmal couldn't help but look at it all.

The scattered skeletons, the white rib bones contrasting the dark landscape blanketed with arrows. Ravens sat atop femurs and skulls. Hollowed frames that once housed families who'd created memories were all forgotten. Gymmal tightened his grip on the reins. The earth would consume Averstone into the ground, but not before vengeance was carried out. For two seasons, the dead remained unsurprisingly patient, anticipating the elfins' return to exact their revenge.

As Gymmal took it all in, Azoria's eyes remained straight ahead. The spirits of Averstone called out to her. The voices had waited a long time to fill Azoria's head with roars of encouragement to avenge them.

She continued on her stomptrodder, stoically riding along. The tougher she acted, the more she suffered inside.

"Do you want to stop by your..." Jandar said, suggesting the obvious.

Azoria raised her hand. "No. Straight to the quarry."

Gymmal was having difficulty keeping his emotions together. There was nothing to compare between the two of them. Azoria had her entire family in her father. He was dead. Gymmal had lost his whole family in the raid. His grandparents had been members of the elder council, his mother had been a teacher, and his father and brother had been builders. It wasn't just who they were, but what they'd done for their neighborhood. Their entire lives dedicated to contributing to a well-functioning community were now meaningless. All for nothing.

"We need to speed up, then," Gymmal said. His demand wasn't just to help Azoria's suffering, but his own. They were moving quickly, but every step seemed like forever to the two survivors.

"I wish we could, but Zuna can't keep up. We need her if we're gonna pull this off," Jandar said.

All Azoria had ever known was torn away from her in the most violent way. The memories of playing with her friends. The comfort of her home. They rushed into her mind like a thunderous storm. Traveling here stabbed at wounds that had never healed. What remained of Averstone was not what they passed through; it was Myra, Sariah, and whoever else may still be alive at the quarry. She would give her life to rescue them.

She looked up, identifying the great constellations that hung over her earth. Brilliant in all their luster, their dancing stars shined bright. "Tira'Sora," She called out. "I haven't prayed much to you. I'm not sure you even know I'm down here. But now I pray that you see me and my hard work. I hope it means something to you. May you grant me strength and protection as I go to save those who love and pray to you more than I ever have."

CHAPTER
Ten

LIGHT THE NIGHT

They made it to the quarry and split up. Azoria and Gymmal waited to enter as Jandar provided overwatch. The young duo sat in the guise of the entrance until two patrol orcs walked by. The cover of night and their darksight gave them an advantage. The path was clear, but only for a short time. Azoria and Gymmal saluted Jandar and Zuna, signaling their departure into the depths of the giant pit. In a flash, they dashed toward the earthen stairway downward and into the quarry's base. They would only have a few minutes to make their way to the cages, which housed approximately two dozen elfins. Across from the two elfin cages were several teen elves tied to giant spikes driven into the ground. Their hands were cuffed in iron shackles with heavy chains connected to the spikes. A few campfires and tents were scattered throughout the quarry, with the cages in the middle. They zig-zagged across the ground, muddied from the diverging creek water running toward the caves at the sides of the pit.

Azoria intensely followed Gymmal, ensuring she stepped in the depressed foot imprints he left to minimize their trace. In between them and the cages were several grimmhound kennels. The hounds were asleep, full of whatever meat they'd devoured from the large bones at their sides. Azoria and Gymmal reapplied their pine needles to their clothes and skin to ensure their scent wouldn't be noticed. The wind started to pick up, creating large whipping ripples that slammed over the orc guard tents. The noise provided cover for their steps toward the cages. Once there, Gymmal split to one cage and used a fetch blade to break the rusted iron lock. Azoria moved to the other cage and did the same with a short knife. She wanted to look up and find Myra but remained concentrated until the lock clicked. Simultaneously, they unfastened the locks and slowly opened the doors. The sleeping elfins sitting against the interior of the cages woke up. They looked at them with wide eyes, disoriented and confused. They were skinny and weak; dirt covered them from head to toe.

"What are you doing? They'll kill us if they see you here," they hissed in uneasy surprise.

"We won't get caught if we go now. Follow us up to the quarry," Azoria ordered.

"No way. The patrol will be here any second. Besides, they killed the last ones who tried to escape!"

Azoria's plan was going differently than she envisioned. The longer they debated, the greater their chances of getting caught. Azoria scanned the area, ensuring they hadn't been detected. "Shhh, lower your voice. Listen, I know you're scared. But do you really plan on living like this forever? Eventually, they'll have no use for you. They'll work you until you die! Let's go!"

Although unsure, the elfins followed nonetheless. As they passed in single file through the cage door and out toward their freedom, Azoria asked, "Where's Myra?"

They shrugged their shoulders and continued exiting. Gymmal's cage was practically empty by then. He made a subtle clicking sound signal that his group was ready to move out. When the final elfin departed, Azoria led the captives toward the steps. She was disheartened but remained faithful that Myra and Sariah were somewhere in these groups. This was no time for loathing. Many elfins trusted her with their lives, and she didn't take the responsibility lightly. She looked up at the ridge for Jandar. He gave signals with a burning branch in his left hand and a large leaf in his right. He covered the flame with the leaf, exposing the flame only in short patterns to give the all-clear. In a long single-file line, they snaked their way through the camp. Azoria led at the head, and Gymmal covered the rear.

As they passed the empty cages, they came across a group of chained teens.

"Get us out of here. Take us with you!" one called out.

"Shhh! They'll hear us, and we'll all end up in shackles," Gymmal said.

"Gymmal, it's me, Ollie!"

Ollie was the leader of the harpy warriors of Averstone. Gymmal knew him as the village bully. But a bully-warrior was precisely what their team needed under the circumstances. Seeing him gave Gymmal a sense of relief and reassurance they could complete the rescue. Gymmal, noticing the line had stopped, decided to try and free them. He ran behind Ollie and used his fetchblade to dig around the giant iron spike that was firmly driven into the ground. Gymmal leveraged his weight against the spike to uproot it, but it barely gave way. "Hurry!" Ollie encouraged as he pulled on the chain in support.

The line began moving ahead, and Gymmal realized that he only had a few critical seconds to help.

"Just free me, and I'll get the rest of them."

"Hold on, I'm trying!" said Gymmal, pulling desperately.

Clumps of dirt covered his blade. He carved a ditch a few inches deep around the spike, exposing a good portion of it. The line was moving quickly by then, and Gymmal had to keep up. "I gotta go, but I hope this helped!"

Ollie nodded in appreciation as he wrapped his chain around the spike and pulled back until it gave way. He ran to his fellow warriors without hesitation and started working on their restraints.

As the line arrived at the stairway, Azoria looked back at Jandar. Jandar gave out the warning signal, waving a leaf over the ember three times, pausing, then three more times. Something was wrong. Jandar noticed a pack of patrol orcs make their way around the opposite side of the ridge and toward the steps. If Azoria and company headed up, they were sure to be captured. Panicked, Azoria froze. She had a line of at least twenty elfins behind her. Any orc who happened to step out of their tent and see this would immediately sound the alarm. Jandar placed the ember down and prepared his bow and arrow.

In the quarry, Azoria briefly considered returning the elves to their cages and returning later.

A little girl behind Azoria spoke. "There's a cave that takes us to the top. I've seen the orcs use it. It's over there." She instantly recognized the voice. It was Sariah. She wanted to ask about Myra, but there was no time to talk. They had to move fast. She sprung toward the dark cave, not knowing what was in it or where it would lead them.

Jandar lost sight of the line when they turned and disappeared to under the left of the ridge. "At least they didn't take the stairs this time," he muttered. Zuna gave out a sigh of relief.

Azoria's eyes adjusted as she entered the dismal cave. With no torches or light sources, it may have been a sign that there were also no orcs. Jandar had taught Azoria that orcs had difficulty seeing in the dark. Eyes forward, she cocked her head a bit to ask Sariah, "Uh, where are we going?"

"We're going the long way." Sariah replied with fear in her voice.

"Great. Anything I should know about this place?"

A third voice in line behind Sariah, spoke. "This is where they keep the green stuff!"

Azoria asked with haste, "What green stuff?"

"The green crystals they make us dig for," Sariah said.

As they turned the corner, a green light shined throughout the domed cavern walls. Standing nearly twenty feet high towered several stacks of brightly glowing ellastrium. It was beautiful. Azoria recalled that the orc she'd battled at the tavern had owned the same green-glowing rock intertwined with his sword.

Gymmal ran toward it. "Remember its use, Zorie! We told Kilajen we would get him some to make his inventions!" He stuffed some into his pant pockets and waistline. Zorie grabbed a few as well. "So, this is the stuff that can harness lightning, huh?"

Sariah tapped Azoria on the shoulder. "What's going on with your sword? I don't think it likes the green stuff."

Azoria removed her sword to discover it was no longer clear. The Klarion was pulsating, violently shifting colors from blue to tones of purple and black. The handle was warm to the touch.

"Gymmal, what do I do?"

"I don't know, but we should probably get out of here."

The next cavern over was more awe-inspiring. Standing in the center was a gigantic gold ring on two iron stands, resembling a mirror, but without reflection. The ring contained a flat surface of the ellastrium, radiating like a green window. The other side was murky. Azoria, caught in a curious trance of sorts, cautiously stepped forward. Wincing, she attempted to peer through it. The light was blinding her elven eyes, which were adjusting to the dark.

"Something's moving in there," she said. "What is this?"

Sariah warned, "There's a human lady who comes here sometimes. She must be important because all the orcs make a big deal of it. They call her the 'majesty.' Anyway, she comes to this room. No one's allowed in here when she's here."

"Zorie, your sword's going crazy again," Gymmal said.

Azoria once again unsheathed the Klarion. "Whatever this is, it doesn't like it."

She looked at the blade, its' handle hot to the touch. The blade itself began to spark, with blue bits of light crackling along the edges. The bevel of the blade's spine glowed florescent blue, and olden elven words were highlighted in silver. Whatever was on the other side of the glass had noticed the blade. It moved closer to the surface. There was a plume of gray smoke floating in a mythical darkness. Behind him, several other smoky figures made their way to the glass. One formed a cloudy limb that contorted into a gray hand, its long nails tapping against the ellastrium. Its eyes were hollowed with green fire in the shape of tunnels leading to a hellish abyss. Its' sharp and twisted teeth like broken, rusted daggers yearning to chew through the ellastrium to feed on the elfins. The figure continued to contort into different shapes and grotesquely smiling.

Azoria lived the last half-year in both terror and anger. The comfort and security of home had forever been shattered, leaving her to wander the dark depths of the forest. The nights where the moonlight hadn't been enough to keep the beasts away. She'd repeatedly been broken by the orcs, whether with her eyes open or closed in her nightmares. But the fear she'd experienced was worldly fear. This was nothing like that. This was the cue of death, something everyone would confront at some point. This was the face of something hungry, with the sole purpose of torturing her. It was as if it longed to end her life and steal her for the hereafter. It was something she couldn't explain, but she knew what it was. Azoria knew it the second she saw it, but could never articulate it. It was in her blood, streamed down from her ancestors. It was a reminder that no matter how pressing our lives were or how distracting it became, something sinister was waiting in the dark. For all her adventures, growth, friendships and failures, she was still only flesh and bone. A true sense of weakness overwhelmed her.

Gymmal and the rest of them felt the uneasiness of the situation. "Zorie, we should go." He calmly nudged her.

She never heard his words. She only heard the ghastly form behind the glass. "Bring me the Klarion," it whispered in a dry, grizzled tone.

Azoria looked at Gymmal. "I need to destroy this thing. It's some kind of portal." The Klarion was heating up, making it hard for her to hold.

"What if the ellastrium is holding it back? Containing it?" Gymmal said.

"No, the ellastrium is bringing it here." She turned and looked at him. "They're mining the ellastrium to make a portal! They're bringing the demons to earth!"

Gymmal pondered for a second. It made sense to him. Whatever those things were, they were stuck on the other side. Someone was calling them to earth. To stop it, there was only one thing to do. "Smash it!" he said. Azoria pressed the Klarion's pommel into her palm.

"*Illuminus shikari*," she said calmly. The sword transformed the sparks around Azoria, and her outline swept into flames of silver and purple. The light from the shift exploded across the cavern.

The elfins huddled in fear, covering their eyes from the light flares. Drenched in silver flames, Azoria felt the rush of energy flow through her body. She pulled back the Klarion and swung at the glass. The first contact created a massive spray of colors across the surface. The demon on the other side floated around, screaming in anger. Azoria swung again, that time with all her might. Shards of ellastrium flung off the mirror as large cracks rippled to the ring's beveled edges. The world behind the glass began to flutter and fade away. The final swing smashed the large portal, raining over twenty feet of ellastrium. The high-pitched shattering sound resonated throughout the caverns. Azoria fell to one knee as Gymmal caught her. Smoke twisted around the cave.

"You did great, Zorie," Gymmal said. "Are you strong enough to keep going? I'm pretty sure someone heard that."

She turned to face him, tears running. "I'm so scared, Gymmal." She rested her head on his shoulder. "Is that where we go when we die? Is that where my mom and dad are?"

It shook Gymmal to see such a vulnerable piece of Azoria. He'd never imagined she had it in her. What they'd all witnessed had introduced them to an evil they'd never known existed.

"I don't think so," he said. "But whatever it is, we're alive right now. So, we must get out of here. Can you lead us?"

Another voice broke through the cave. "Azoria!" An elfin from the back of the line stood up, waving and moving forward. "Zorie! It's me!"

Azoria recognized her voice at the first syllable. "Myra?" she said. "Myra!" She raised up in disbelief and then ran for a hug.

"Look at you! You did all of this?" Myra shouted in shock and relief. "I knew it! If anyone was going to rescue us, it would be you!"

Azoria examined Myra, her long dirty hair, her thin frame. "Sariah guided us out. Did they hurt you? Are you okay?" she asked.

"I'm fine, Zorie, I promise. Everything's gonna be fine now that you're here!"

"I missed you, my friend! I thought about you every day, hoping you survived. When Gymmal told me you were here, there was no way we weren't coming to get you." Azoria turned to the rest of the elfins. "All of you. Let's get you to safety!"

Relieved, Azoria felt a surge of optimism. She was more motivated than ever to get out of this dingy world and go back to having fun with her best friend. That's all she'd wanted since the beginning. "I'll take the lead," Azoria said as she returned to the front of the line.

Thanks to Sariah's directions, they discovered a tight scuttle running at a forty-five-degree angle that could bring them to the surface. The night sky was viewable from their viewpoint. It was some type of ventilation for the cavern, and the elfins would have to climb to make it out. It was just wide enough for one elfin to fit at a time.

The Klarion returned to a dimly pulsating blue hue, just giving the line of escapees enough light to move through the tunnel. At the other end, they could hear orc voices. Gymmal was too far behind to offer any guidance. The elfins were getting restless, standing in the small foxhole.

Azoria was nervous. Fear shot through her veins, freezing her in her tracks. She realized the gravity of the situation. The orcs at the exit would surely call for reinforcements if they were seen. Worse yet, the elves could be trapped in the scuttle from both ends.

Meanwhile, Jandar remained at the top of the ridge, and the patrol orc he was keeping an eye on was returning to check on the cages at the quarry base. Jandar pressed the arrow against his face as he pulled the bowstring back. In his line of sight, he locked on the patrol orc. That's when he noticed his guide hand shaking. He'd ignored the urge to drink all day, and his body was beginning to protest.

Along with the aches and pains that came with midlife, he was finding it hard to maintain his pose. A shot like this wouldn't have been a challenge in his younger days. Now, he just prayed his wrist or elbow didn't lock up. But he had the orc in his sights. He accepted his purpose and was disciplined enough to turn as still as a stone statue when needed. He pushed the shaky hand and the pains out of his mind and regained his focus. *Not today*, he thought. The voices begging for a cold ale vanished from his head. He swallowed slowly and steadied his breathing. Jandar was back.

"Don't do it," he whispered, as if warning the orc through telepathy. It was no use. The orc made a double take of the cage. Once he realized the cages were empty, the orc reached for the horn around his neck to sound the alarm. Jandar pulled the bow back a touch further, calculating the distance the arrow would need to connect to its target. As the orc raised the horn to his lips, Jandar released the arrow. As the orc exhaled, a sharp, high-pitched sound clambered through the horn. It lasted barely a second as the arrow sliced directly into the horn and through the orc's mouth. The arrowhead poked from the back of his neck.

Although a perfect shot, the orc didn't fall. He struggled to yank the arrow out of his open mouth. In a state of panic, the orc turned to run. Jandar cursed, quickly retrieving another arrow. Like his shadow ranger days, he slung the blow string back and immediately fired another arrow in one swift motion. It was so fast; he saw it connect with the orc before the bowstring reset. The arrow ripped into his left eye, collapsing the orc. It was a perfect shot, but there was no celebration. The orc's body lay close enough to the cages that any guard at the camp could easily see it. "Damnit!" he cursed.

Meanwhile, Azoria had no choice but to charge out of the foxhole. At the other end, she could see them; two orcs. She withdrew the Klarion again, readying herself for a surprise attack. A faint horn cracked through the air as she moved toward the figures. It ended just as quickly as it had begun. The orcs turned to scamper toward horn's call in the quarry. Azoria rushed out of the foxhole, confirming a clear path. The mouth of the scuttle opened into a flat, open field surrounded by forest. She motioned for the elfins to come out, slowly exiting one after another. She pointed at the stars and told them to run until they reached a stream. Then, follow the stream north.

To her back, each elf raced across the open field and into the woods. "Follow the moon. You'll see a stream. Take the stream north," Azoria instructed, bracing for any sudden visitors.

Myra broke the line to hug Azoria. "Thank you, sister."

Azoria, with her sword at her side, said, "You should go. I'll see you soon."

As they hugged, Myra whispered, "I told you one day you'd do something really important. I always believed in you."

Azoria smiled. "I know you have. Thank you."

A sudden thud pushed Myra violently into Azoria. Myra's hands dropped, and all her weight lay over Azoria. Unable to support her weight, Azoria stumbled back.

Horrified, Azoria looked down to see an arrowhead sticking out from Myra's chest. A loud horn sounded as the forest awoke, with several orcs bursting from the tree line before her. More arrows coasted in Azoria's direction. Before she could process the situation, an arrow struck her left shoulder. She whipped backward as she lost all feeling in her left arm. Falling over Myra, Azoria screamed in a mixture of rage and anguish.

Jandar continued to pick off his orcs at the camp. He'd dropped three in the quarry base, but now there were too many to count. He was sure they'd spotted where his arrows were raining from. One raised their horn to alert the horde of orcs scattered throughout the quarry. To his left, his ears absorbed a ghastly scream. It was Azoria. Without thinking, he and Zuna leaped over his earthen bunker and sprinted to Azoria.

As more arrows poured over the elfin, Gymmal crouched in front of Azoria and raised his bracer to deflect them. The orcs were quickly coming upon Gymmal. He had just enough time to remove his fetchers and form a cross over his head. The closest orc swung his axe down onto Gymmal's fetchers. Too heavy, the orc's momentum caved over Gymmal. He rolled off his hips and tossed the orc off balance. As the orc stumbled to the ground, Gymmal threw his left fetcher at another incoming orc. The blades released and sunk into the orc's chest, immediately dropping him. His battle axe sputtered outside his hand and into the dirt. Down to one fetcher, Gymmal realized he wouldn't get the other back without leaving Azoria. The first orc that had rolled to the ground was coming to, already up onto his knees. Just a few feet away, Gymmal lunged toward him and stabbed him in his throat. The orc fell forward, grabbing his neck. Two others were charging toward him. With one fetcher left, Gymmal knew he could take one and fight empty-handed against the other. Then, he decided to try to boomerang it. He threw the fetcher. It sliced through the first one's bow, rendering its range weapon useless. As the other reloaded, Gymmal swiftly recovered the returning fetcher and slung it back out. That time, it stuck into the orc's arm. The orc dropped his bow and held his arm in pain.

The elfins were in the forest by then, but Gymmal had to buy more time. He was empty-handed against the remaining orc, who'd switched from his broken bow to a sword. In the background, he could hear more orcs approaching their location. Gymmal searched around and saw the battle axe. It was heavy, but he mustered the strength to pick it up. He charged toward the readying orc. No sooner had he taken his first step, another round of arrows whizzed past his head—that time toward the orcs. It was Jandar. He shot off several arrows at one time, quickly dropping the two remaining orcs. Gymmal released the heavy axe and scavenged for his fetchers.

"Let's go!" Jandar said as he rushed to Azoria. Her left sleeve was soaked in blood, and she was growling in anger, like something had been awakened from deep in her bowels.

"Myra. You killed Myra," she mumbled repeatedly.

"We gotta go, Zorie," Gymmal said. He placed her on Zuna's back, and they sprinted off. Soon, several more orcs entered the area, combing through the forest.

Leading the way was a familiar-looking orc. He had braids in the shape of mohawk, a necklace of ears and a collection of bracelets on his arms. "I want those rodents back. Search the whole forest, burn it down if you must."

It wasn't close, but Jandar and company found a spot to catch their breath and think up a plan. "The elfins went this way. If the orcs are sweeping the area, they will end up between us and the elfins. They'll cut us off from them. We need to get to them before they do."

"We told them to meet us at the creek, so that's where they're headed," Gymmal said.

"Azoria's out of it. We need to get her to safety as well. We can't afford to run into these guys again." Azoria was shaking, still whispering to herself with streams of tears. She laid over Zuna, who was eager to get moving. She could smell the wretched stench of the orcs moving closer. She whimpered in worry.

"We have no choice; we need to split up. Zuna, take Zorie away from here, deeper into the woods." He kneeled and scratched Zuna's nose. "Follow the creek upstream." Zuna yipped in concurrence. "Gymmal, you and I will go to the elfins and take them upstream to meet up with Zuna."

"What if they catch her before we get there?" asked Gymmal.

"Zuna's faster than anything out there. She should have no problems heading up."

Zuna raced off while Jandar and Gymmal pushed through the forest. Through the night, they could hear the sounds of orcs commanding orders and grimmhounds tracking through the foliage. As they made their way over a steep hill, they saw dozens of bright torches contrasting against the dark ground. Some orcs were being pulled by their ravenous grimmhounds. The orcs had already cut between them. Jandar, who never fell to defeat easily, looked at the pattern of trees that towered over the orcs. "Can you climb, kid?"

Gymmal gave Jandar a look of shock. "I guess, a little."

"Good enough." Jandar took to the nearest tree and shifted himself upward. Pieces of bark chipped off and dropped over Gymmal as he covered his eyes from the falling debris. Gymmal followed, pulling himself up to the first branch, and then the second. Before he knew it, he was nearly twenty feet above the ground. The branches from the trees ahead were touching, allowing him and Jandar to climb across about like a bridge. As the hill receded below, they found themselves higher in the sky. Jandar stopped to allow Gymmal to keep up, but Gymmal was trembling in fear. The grimmhounds below picked up their scents and started barking in excitement. Gymmal froze, realizing just how high up he was. The breeze was pushing the branches, making them more unstable and unpredictable. The wind whooshing against trees sounded like ocean waves, sending leaves fluttering. Gymmal, on his stomach, tightly hugged the branch and watched a leaf twist down.

The reality set in that any sudden slip, and he could drop faster than the leaves. "Snap out of it. Think about the elfins." Jandar's voice broke his hypnosis.

It was easier said than done. As Jandar looked forward again, he could feel the eerily familiar tickle of a spider's soft feet stepping over his arm. There it was, approximately the size of his hand. It was furry, with all its black marbly eyes focused on Jandar. There were so many eyes, and Jandar refused to look at any of them. His heart beat strong enough to vibrate the mighty tree branch. The spider crept a few paces forward, its sharp jaws shifting around.

"What's the problem? I thought we were moving," Gymmal whispered from behind.

Jandar shook his head in disbelief as if trying to wake himself up. The spider's jerky movements dazed him. He was paralyzed with fear, and Gymmal's words of encouragement echoed somewhere outside his tunnel of panic. The only one who could revive Jandar was Jandar. *Come on,* he told himself. *This one isn't poisonous. It can't hurt you like the big one did. Keep going. Do it for Azoria.*

Jandar coached himself back to reality. He never noticed that the tarantula had moved on more than a minute ago. Jandar realized he hadn't breathed in about the same amount of time. Flushed, he sucked in as much air as he could. The breeze picked up again, but they climbed on.

AZORIA OPENED HER EYES WHEN SHE CAUGHT THE SOUND OF RUNNING water. She and Zuna were just a few feet from the creek. Zuna sat her down, leaving a large blood smear across her back. Azoria limped over and splashed water across her shoulder. The wind grew loud, howling so loud that it perked Zuna's ears. The gale carried the voices of the orcs scouring the forest. Zuna was disoriented. She was unable to determine how far away the voices were or which direction they were coming from. She nuzzled at Azoria, signaling that they needed to start moving again. Azoria was dazed. She'd bled out so much that she only had her anger to keep her on her feet. She couldn't believe she waited seasons to finally see Myra again, just to lose her instantly. There was no time to talk, no celebration, no uplifting ending. Her mother and father were dead, and her best friend inched toward a simular fate. Zuna's chatter to direct them to move quickly increased to growls. Sounds of water splashing downstream caught her attention. Their chance to escape had evaded them. Light from torches radiated behind the rocks. It was too late. Even though Zuna could sprint away, there was no way she could leave her wounded friend alone. Even if it meant death. Azoria bent to Zuna and pet her with her good arm.

"Leave, girl. I'm finishing this."

Zuna was unmovable. She'd made her pact. She was staying. Both were of far different species, but each had lost so much. They were refugees who'd made their new life in the forest. Azoria brandished her Klarion with her good arm and stepped in front of Zuna. The dire wolf turned toward Azoria's side, both facing whatever was coming out next. Around the bank came two grimmhounds, red fiery eyes and smoky nostrils charging toward them. Both were a bit smaller than Zuna, but together, the odds were in their favor. They barked as they sped faster toward the elfin and the wolf. They were hard to see, as their black coats were dark as shadows. Azoria let out a scream that shook the ground. She swung down on the first one in a devastating fashion. The hound rolled over itself and dropped, lifeless. Azoria met the other one as she reset her sword in a ready position and cut it nearly in half. The blade glowed a brighter blue as it easily slid through the hound.

Her left arm was still dangling by her side. Blood dripped down her fingertips. She let out another yell and raised the Klarion with her right hand as the orcs turned the corner to confront her. Zuna drew back on her haunches, her tail stiff. Three orcs presented themselves, slowing from a jog to a walk.

"You're gonna pay for my hounds, runt," one orc said. Zuna barked, shaking the ground. The orcs encircled her and fixed their eyes on the glowing blue sword.

Azoria was conflicted. Jandar's voice warned her not to use her powers recklessly. Nashara and Kilajen advised her to use the blade solely for its intentions. She shook her head. These were the same orcs who'd destroyed her home. Their dark green skin, snout-like noses. She was half the size of one of the orcs, and one arm was useless. There was no way she would be able to take them alone on in her state. But once again, her rage was taking over. A mixture of blood, dirt, and tears painted her face. There was no fear that time.

She knelt and used her left knee to lay her injured hand on. She pressed her thumb on the thorn until it bled. With everything she had, she roared out, "*Illuminus shikari!*" The blue light beamed from the sword as smoke shot from around her. Her outline glared in silver and her eyes rolled back, revealing the metallic sheen. Within an instant, her silver flames moved across her silhouette. A charge of air entered Azoria, as if she had never breathed before. Her left arm felt new as she grabbed the handle with both hands. She rose to her feet, standing taller than before, practically equal to the orc's height.

One of the orcs screamed in shock. Panicked, he turned to run. The other two clenched their heavy swords and ran toward Azoria. She met them first, striking the closest one with the blade before he could swing forward. The blade went cleanly through him. He fell immediately to his knees. Standing in front of him, she raised her leg and pushed his body off the sword. The other orc was at her left side when she turned 180 degrees and sliced his attacking arm off. Before he could take another step, his severed arm dropped to the ground, leaving sporadic blotches of blood staining the ground. She charged her right shoulder into his chest as he was flung onto his back. He screamed with the realization that he would bleed out soon. No longer a threat, she stepped over him as he begged for help. Zuna, a relatively quick dire wolf, had momentarily lost track of Azoria during her dizzying attack. She quickly met Azoria's side and followed her down the creek. Surrounded in a cocoon of shimmering lights, Azoria moved as if being carried by the winds.

JANDAR AND GYMMAL REACHED THE BANK TO FIND BODIES LYING ON THE forest floor. "Damnit, Azoria," Jandar said as he examined the scene.

Gymmal looked around. "Why 'Damnit, Azoria?'"

"These are fresh. The blood, the bodies. It was her. The wounds were cauterized as it was cut through. I can also smell it in the air. She must have shifted. Tracks show three orcs, but there's only two bodies. She's hunting the third one."

Gymmal asked with obvious worry, "What do we do? We can't leave the kids."

"That's right. But we can't leave Azoria. Her power doesn't last very long. When it runs out, she's going to be exhausted. I gotta go after her. You go get the children and take them to the trail. Don't wait for us. Just head back toward Ceresbow."

"Remember the last time I tried to save the kids? Didn't end so well for me." Gymmal said.

"You were different then. I witnessed a strong man defending those he cares about tonight. A warrior, dangerous and proficient in his newfound fetchblades. You did that. And I know you'll honor your people and protect those elfins."

Gymmal nodded and began running upstream. "Jandar, please save her."

"Deal." Jandar rushed after the burn trails scorched in the ground. The more he followed, the more bodies he came upon. He counted six by the time he reached Azoria. She was kneeling with her sword propping her up, the silver flames dim and vanishing into the night. Zuna ran back to Jandar, as if afraid of something.

"Azoria, Gymmal's taking the elfins to the stomptrotters. We did it. We need to get out of here."

"I'm not done yet, Jandar. I saw the orc from the tavern. He proudly wears the bracelet of my clan, like a trophy. I must finish this."

"Zorie, listen to me. There'll be time for that later. Our mission was to bring the kids back."

"Back to where? Their homes were charred to stilts. So is yours. There's nothing to go back to. We have nothing."

"Azoria, I can rebuild. We can rebuild."

"Not until I spill blood."

Jandar remained quiet, witnessing Azoria's heroic potential to turn into something more evil than what she hunted. Her rage grew more insatiable with each body she cut down.

He yelled at her as she continued to march. "You have something most of us don't. You have a purpose! Do you see the gifts your ancestors left you? You don't see it now, but one day you will. They allowed you to protect others so they don't suffer the same fate. Without you, all our sacrifices mean nothing."

Azoria remained quiet. His words were impactful and pushed her to think outside of her selfish cause.

"Azoria, you still have Gymmal. You have Razzle and Nashara. Zorie, you have me."

Azoria ran the tiny arches of her thumb's fingerprint against the sharp thorn spike. The point teased and tickled against her skin, as if summoning her blood. The death of so many orcs at her hands felt satisfying. She enjoyed it.

"I want more justice," she muttered in such a low tone that Jandar barely recognized her.

"This isn't justice, kid. This is bloodlust."

She felt compelled to push down on the thorn and finish the job. Her energy was drained and her knees weakened, she was close to fainting. She breathed in heavily, trying to catch her breath. "I hate them all, Jandar. I want them all to die."

There was sorrow in Jandar's heart. He empathized with her. But there was also a trickle of fear. She would only continue to grow.

Being so young and having the ability to annihilate anyone who got in her way with an uncontrollable rage had the word 'danger' written all over it. It was too much responsibility for an adult, let alone a child.

"If you can't control this now, then you'll never be satisfied. I knew your mom and dad. Trust me, they wouldn't want this."

His words echoed in her mind. It was true, her father would have been disappointed. She'd taken lives. Green bodies lay about, limbs separated from torsos. The true horrors had been cloaked under the cover of night. Who was she? What had she done? What had she turned into? Azoria was no better than the orcs. As she calmed herself, the hunger for more blood subsided. The little twelve-year-old elfin girl returned. She was ashamed.

Azoria rose, tired and in pain. Every inch of her body suffered. As she limped over to Jandar, he sprinted over to her and gave her a hug. There it was. All that either of them had ever truly wanted; family. He had his little niece back. She had her family. It was familiar, yet foreign to her. A part of her had died when Averstone died. Azoria didn't believe she could find peace within or outside of herself again. She squeezed him tighter, releasing a barrage of warm tears, surprising Jandar. She used him to hug her mother and father. Her screams resonated in his chest. She'd never cried like that before. Six long months of torture had been confined inside of her. Jandar stood there, like the rock she needed. He had no words to give, no advice or training. He stayed silent. For just a moment, she let some of it out. Her guard was down just enough to release an inkling of trauma. Then she breathed in heavily and cleared her throat, trying to compose herself. She was ready to leave.

THE CHILDREN AND TEENS HOVERED OVER MYRA, WHO BLED SO HEAVILY they could no longer distinguish between the ground and her body.

Azoria had no strength left. She fell to her knees and took Myra's cold hands.

"I can't save my sister, Zorie," Sariah cried. "I'm so sorry."

Jandar, once again assuming watch, ushered Gymmal and Ollie to help keep an eye out. Zuna lay at Azoria's side.

"The moonlight isn't enough to draw my healing power."

"The sun won't be up for another couple of hours. She'll be gone by then," one of the harpies reluctantly admitted.

Azoria wept quietly to herself, her body trembling to hold it inside. The tears seeped out of her eyes as she softly hummed to calm herself down. It was her mother's song.

"Wait," Gymmal said. "Sariah, you said you need a powerful light source."

It suddenly hit Azoria, who was nearly lying next to Myra. She looked up at Sariah. "Would my power be enough to draw from?"

"Azoria, no. You're not strong enough. Shifting more might kill you," Jandar warned, still searching the perimeter for incoming orcs.

His worry was in vain because it was of no matter to Azoria. She ignored him and asked Sariah again.

"I don't know. Maybe... maybe not." Sariah shrugged.

"There's only one way to find out. Help pull me up." A few elfins and harpies helped bring Azoria to her feet. She stabilized herself as the pain rapidly returned to her left shoulder. It wouldn't be much longer until her left arm regressed to being useless once more, so she had to work fast. The kids crowded around her, encouraging her. Jandar could see the torches moving forward through the trees before him. He could feel three bows remaining in his quiver. There was a far greater number of orcs. He knew the engagement was imminent the moment Azoria lit up. There wasn't much else to discuss.

Jandar looked back at Ollie. "We need to bring the fight to them. Keep them as far away from Azoria as possible," he said. Ollie and his crew nodded. They rushed toward Jandar in support. It was unspoken that they were sacrificing their lives to save one of their own.

For all their flaws and juvenile behavior, Ollie and his team had good in them. Azoria appreciated it.

"If you're going to shift, you better do it now." Jandar charged forward, followed by the small band. Zuna circled around the kids like a protective mother.

Azoria looked at Sariah, thinking of something her father once told her. "Light is hope. If even the tiniest glimmer of light exists, then so does hope."

Sariah smiled.

Azoria looked at Sariah. "I believe in you. We gotta do this for Myra. I know she believes in you. I'll try if you try, okay?"

Sariah shook her head in approval. "Okay, Zorie. I'll try."

"Alright, Clair," Azoria said to her sword. "Just one more time."

Jandar didn't see the transformation, but the reflection of the explosion lit up the forest for a few seconds. As the orcs turned toward the action, Jandar and the team rushed them. There was no time to count the number of enemies or to come up with a strategy.

"*Acha!* Stone Harpies, attack!" Ollie said as they all let out high-pitched screeches like eagles. The sound confused the enemy. Through the brush charged the harpies, wildly swinging their weapons with no regard for their opponents in front of them.

As Ollie pounced on the first one, the warriors followed, choosing their closest target and smashing into a few unsuspected orcs. To their right, Gymmal launched both of his fetchblades, knocking two orcs over. Standing on top of a lifeless body, Jandar presented his bow and managed to take down another orc. While several went down quickly, there were more waves of orcs. The element of surprise was fading, and he knew how quickly the tide of the skirmish would turn.

With everything she had left, Azoria reignited into the shikari. That time, it didn't seem as bright or powerful as before. Little Sariah closed her eyes and reached her hands out in front of Azoria, trying to absorb her light. Her palms turned a brilliant orange, a sign that it was working. Sariah opened her eyes, which also matched the orange color of her palms. Azoria concentrated, trying to keep her flame alight for as long as she could. The remainder of the elfins were younger than Azoria, and far smaller.

"You heard what the guy said, protect Azoria at all costs!" one small elfin cried out. They all ran toward Zuna, picking up anything they deemed could be a weapon; rocks and branches. Standing together, they remained vigilant as they heard the battle taking place in front of them.

Fatigue was setting in, and Jandar was losing his speed. For each orc he took down, another slipped past him and toward the elfins. When Jandar turned to run after him, an orc collided into him, slamming him to the ground. Scraped up, Jandar pushed himself back onto his feet, but the orc managed to throw a fist that sent him back down. The world was spinning around him. He was conscious enough to know what was happening, but his body ignored the will to stand back up. By then, a second orc had arrived, that time swinging a mace at his arm. Jandar tried to block, only to absorb the full force of the blow, sending him back a few feet and tumbling to the ground.

Ollie and the other teens were no match for the orcs. The green giants barreled their way through them, pummeling them against rocks and trees. One orc was not interested in the wasting time fighting the warriors. He casually stepped over many of the harpies' battered bodies and marched toward Jandar. Gymmal was finding success with a few of the orcs. He was building a rhythm to his attack, being just quick enough to avoid their heavy punches that were like battering rams. Only a handful of warriors remained on their feet.

The bigger orc picked up Jandar by his collar and lifted him off his feet to eye level. "You've been an annoying bug, ranger. You're the one from the tavern! Are you responsible for all of this?"

Jandar, broken and unable to speak, used the last of his breath to spit blood in the orc's face. Only able to see out of one eye, Jandar gave a partial smile, exposing the blood coating his teeth. The orc snorted. "Tonight, we take no prisoners. Kill them all. Start with this one." The big orc dropped him to the ground like a sack of trash as the others walked toward Jandar to finish him. Gymmal and another warrior rushed to intercept them. As the bigger orc made his way toward the flames, Gymmal tossed his fetchblades out at the orcs advancing on Jandar.

"Bring it, hogs." Jandar raised his arms and clenched his fists in a wobbly boxing pose. "I don't have much left, but I'm sure there's just enough to handle you."

Gymmal was too busy with one orc to notice the other. That orc moved toward Jandar with a longsword in hand. Jandar possessed to much spirit to accept the hopelessness of his situation. He figured as long as he was on his feet, there was a fighting chance. Just as the oncoming orc raised his sword, a small arrow slid into his neck. He dropped his sword and turned to see who'd gotten him.

As he spun around, a fist met his left temple, sending him crashing to the ground. Jandar tried to open his good eye in disbelief and stumbled back. The defender's hand caught him before he fell, exposing a small crossbow strapped to his forearm.

"Easy there, old man. Looks like you've seen better days." It was Colvin. "You owe me too much for me to lose you like this."

Meanwhile, Azoria was losing focus. Her energy was draining, and the flames were frantically dissipating.

"Here we go!" one of the elfins cautiously yelled in anticipation as orcs began approaching from out of the dark forest.

"Go away, monkey-pigs!" one of the elfins yelled. "We're not going back to the camp!"

"Don't worry. You won't be alive to go back," one said.

Zuna howled. This may be her last stand as well. Even though she was a large, powerful wolf, she was unsure of her ability to fight against an orc. She pushed off the ground and leaped onto the closest one. He swung at her with his sword, but she was too quick. Her weight and thrust sent him crashing onto the ground. Before he could reach for his knife, she'd already dug her fangs into his neck. After she finished him, she raised her head to see two more creeping out of the tree-line. The taste of blood filled her with a surge of energy. She rushed toward them.

Gymmal made his way to Jandar and Colvin. "You took quite a licking."

Jandar, loudly snorting through the blood just to breathe, raised his right arm and gave a thumbs up. "Most of this isn't mine."

Colvin laughed. "Wishful thinking, old man."

Jandar's good eye began to close. "Speaking of old man, I'm just going to take a short nap. I'll be there in a minute."

Colvin sat him against a tree.

"I'll come back and check up on you," Gymmal said.

"Sure thing." Jandar was able to say three words before closing his eyes. "Go save Zorie."

Just as Gymmal made his way to the open field, so did the largest of the orcs. He had a wide sword in his right hand, dragging it on the ground behind him. *This must be the leader*, Gymmal thought. Zuna had finished the last of the soldier orcs as her eyes set on the incoming one. She growled intensely as the blood ran over her dark blue coat.

"Sir Gortrog." The dying orc struggled to speak under Zuna's weight, desperately raising his arm. "Save me."

Gortrog paid him no mind. He was furiously stepping over the bodies of his army scattered about. Seeing that a wolf, a ranger, and a few children could cause this type of damage didn't make sense to him. But when he locked his eyes on Azoria, it all came together for him. The light radiating from her instantly blinded Gortrog. He covered his eyes with his other hand and squinted. "You! The blade wielder!"

"Get back!" One elfin threw a rock, barely reaching him.

Gortrog raised his sword, giving no attention to the little ones. He was fixated on Azoria. "I remember that little runt. It'll be a pleasure to finally kill you."

He activated the ellastrium in his heavy sword by pushing it farther into the blade's groove. Green sparks of lightning sprayed out of the blade. He marched toward Azoria, her back facing him. Gymmal threw a fetchblade with all his might to stop Gortrog. It spun at an incredible speed, so fast, it made a whistle sound cutting through the air. Gortrog nonchalantly raised his sword over his face, blocking the sharp ends from making contact. Gymmal followed through with the second one while running toward him. As the other one spun out, he picked up the first one. He finally got Gortrog's attention, taking his first swing at the incoming elfin. Zuna rushed Gortrog from the other side.

Azoria was shaking uncontrollably. The flames had softened, but she managed to continue, focused. Just when she was losing it, she thought back to her mother, her grandmother, and the women who'd come before them. She realized that she'd wasted her energy in anger and could now put it to good use. Instead of blocking the pain, she accepted it. Then, she channeled her pain to fuel her hope. The flames brightened outward again, pulling into Sariah's hands. The sword could only do so much, but it was Azoria who was making this happen. The flames shot out from her like a silver phoenix. A surge of emotions spun through her, and the energy recharged. The flames became stronger, crackling and waving so loudly in her ears that she could not hear anything happening around her.

In her trance, she was oblivious to the violence Gortrog was inflicting against her allies. Zuna flung across a giant rock. Her leg snapped, and she was unable to move. Gymmal crumbled onto the ground with a large gash over his chest. Lightning projected from Gortrog's broadsword poured over the elfins as they screamed in pain.

Sariah's little hands looked as if they were on fire. She lightly placed them on Myra's temples. *Sister, come back to us*, Sariah pleaded to herself. The light brightened across Myra's body, and an orange glow encompassed them. There was a twitch in Myra's fingers. Her chest arched up, as if fighting for air. Immediately, her eyes opened, and she sucked in a huge breath. The wound on her chest began to close as she smiled at the awe of the aurora standing over her. It reminded her of some kind of guardian angel. Before she could call out to Azoria, a giant green flash of light shot out behind her. Azoria fell forward, but braced herself from hitting the ground. She turned and saw Gortrog in front of her.

"Sister!" Utilizing the burst of adrenaline, Myra scrambled to her feet and picked up Sariah to avoid the fight.

Azoria covered their escape back to the woods. Gortrog slashed at Azoria, but she parried, causing another spark of lighting that brilliantly mixed in contrasting colors. They pushed against each other, their swords crossed and their eyes meeting. Azoria could see his forearm pressed against the sword, displaying the many bracelets of his victims. Then, she saw her father's.

They clashed again. His broadsword did not shatter like the others. Azoria was surprised by the durability of his weapon. She figured it was one Kilajen had forged. There was no time to contemplate. Stepping back, she noticed his necklace, with dozens of elven ear tips haphazardly sewn as pendants.

Gortrog was stronger than the other orcs, and surprisingly quick. Gortrog realized this was a different Azoria to the one he'd encountered long ago at the tavern. She spun back. Because her sword was much shorter, she knew that thrusting at him would be futile. She had to rely on her speed and smaller stature to slide under his sword and attack.

He swung again, missing her as she ducked. But his sword battered through an old tree, slicing it in half. As the top of the tree fell over, Myra quickly moved herself and Sariah away. Gortrog lunged forward. It was the moment Azoria had been waiting for. As she dived under his strike, she used her blade to run through his right upper thigh. The blade melted through his muscle and to the bone. Gortrog let out a yell that shook the ground as he fell over his right leg. Partly down, he connected at her back, that time throwing her against the dirt. She rolled a few times and rose back up. Even through her protected flames, it was now evident that she could be injured. She'd felt every bit of his swing. Her right shoulder blade was torn open, exposing a deep red gash.

This had to end quickly, as her concentration was breaking. The once spectacularly bright flames around her that fought to exist were now quickly fanning out. Gortrog swung his sword out again in a sweeping motion. She blocked, but she could feel the brute force of his power. Both of them were severely injured. Gortrog was no longer able to walk. Having the advantage, she swung downward toward him. He placed his sword in front of himself as it absorbed the impact. Again, she swung down, and he fell back further. She continued to swing, one after another. Each time, dropping him a bit more. She didn't want him to die too quickly. Azoria wanted him to feel the imminent force of death in the pit of his stomach, much like her father must have felt.

Gortrog was exhausted. He would become too weak to raise his sword. All he could do was yell out in protest. As Azoria swung again, she heard the voice of her best friend gently whisper, "Zorie, you got him. He can't hurt you anymore." Azoria paused from her axing and looked back at Myra. "It's okay. You've done it. You've saved us."

Azoria looked down at herself. The flames had long sputtered out. Her body burned from the damage she'd taken in battle. Every cut stung. She realized she was standing in her own blood. Her energy was gone and her body flushed. Azoria sucked in as much air as she could, trying to slow down her breathing. Then she peered across the field. There were so many lifeless bodies sprawled about. Meaningless pockets of death. The sounds of agony from the injured stretched over the battlefield.

She quickly inspected Clair. The sword looked as clean as it had the first time she'd been introduced to it in her mother's chest back home. Unlike Azoria, Clair remained brilliant and shiny. However, her light was dimming. *Is it finally satisfied?* Azoria thought to herself.

Just as she thought it was the end, noise from many individuals pushing past bushes and branches shook the trees in front of her.

There were several steps, meaning several more beings moving out of the forest and toward the elfins. Myra gasped as Azoria tried to lift Clair. But it was too much for her little worn-out frame to muster. "Damnit, it's still not over," she slurred. There were too many figures exiting the forest and into the tall grass. "I can't do this anymore." Azoria dropped to both knees and let out a soft cry. "Acha! Tira'So-ra! Kill me, then. If you're not satisfied, then just get it over with! I can't do it again." She lowered her head in despair and closed her eyes, squeezing them as the tears sputtered out. Myra and Sariah crawled to her in comfort. "They keep coming. What more do they want?" Azoria wept.

The beings showed themselves under the moonlight through the tall grass a few yards away. It was Ollie and the surviving teens. They'd made it, limping badly out of the woods. Jandar was with them, leaning against one of them like a crutch. Azoria was over-whelmed with relief. She raised her head and cried with joy.

The bunches of injured elves hobbled toward each other slowly, as every motion felt unbearable. Ollie and the warriors looked over at Gortrog. He yelled in orc while spitting his blood at the elves.

"He'll come back," Sariah said. "I don't want to see him in my nightmares anymore."

"Worry no more, little one. He's defeated. I say we kill him so he can't go back and tell anyone about this," Ollie said.

"No, Ollie. The mission's complete. We saved the elfins. You res-cued your friends. That portal's been destroyed," Gymmal contest-ed, lying on his side. "There's been enough killing. Look around us. Killing him doesn't change anything."

Ollie and the other warriors raised their spears and circled Gor-trog, looking down and yelling back at him in elven. Gortrog was barely concious but raised his sword in defiance as his leg pumped out streams of blood. Azoria recognized Ollie's words. It was the chants of the hunting party. They sang their traditional song after a good kill.

Azoria mustered the last of her strength and rose. She looked directly into Gortrog's stony eyes. "I remember when a pack of wolves attacked a giant bear. I watched the whole thing. It fought for hours. It even killed a few wolves. Those wolves knowingly sacrificed themselves for the good of their kin. The bear wanted to keep fighting, but after many hours, it slowed down. It limped around in circles with two wolves clinging to its hump. Finally, it laid down, as if accepting its fate. The bear didn't die immediately. The wolves ate it for hours, clearing the backside first and then into the ribs. It just sat there, surprisingly still. It was as if it was offering itself to them."

The warriors poked at Gortrog with the spears in a toying fashion. They took their time, jabbing the tips through his thick flesh. He parried a few but was too weak to give any real effort. Their song become louder, ensuring it would be the last thing his ears would absorb. He'd lost so much blood.

Azoria continued to stare. Then she pointed at him. "You are the bear."

"I declare we kill him. If we let him live, he'll come back with another army. The next one will be bigger," Ollie said.

"It doesn't matter whether you kill him or not. They're going to come. They're not coming with an army. They'll come with a storm," Jandar mumbled through his fractured jaw.

Azoria, with her flames finally extinguished, turned to hug Myra. She needed something, and it wasn't revenge. She just wanted her friend. Nothing needed to be said. She was safe.

Ollie scoffed. "Are you kidding me? They butchered our homes, killed our parents! I say he dies!"

"And give him an honorable death? These orcs prefer to die in battle. Killing him will only fulfill their blood oath," Jandar said, holding the side of his face.

"The half-breed is right. I will come back. And I'll bring the might of two kingdoms with me! The Varosians and ScurGard. All of us!" yelled Gortrog. "You will hide, but we will hunt you all down and kill you with nothing more than a thought. Crosslands will be ours. The sorceress queen will—"

As the last word escaped his lips, Ollie drove his spear down, behind Gortrog's skull and into his back. He struggled briefly as Ollie twisted the spear further into him. Gortrog reached for the spear behind him. He snorted as his back cracked apart. He fought for a few gasps of air as blood shot from his eyes and nose. He gurgled as the spear ran deeper through his backside, parallel to his spine. It protruded out of the skin of his lower back and continued into the ground. Ollie shifted the spear around as the sound of cracking filled everyone's ears. Gortrog's arms retired to his side and his head slung down. The elfins screamed in disgust. Jandar solemnly looked on.

"What did you do!" Gymmal yelled angrily.

"You idiot! He mentioned a sorceress queen. He was about to tell us something!" Azoria said.

"What's it matter?" Ollie said. "I tire of his words!" He lashed out at everyone watching. "Azoria might be satisfied, but I crave to have my fill! She didn't sit in captivity for almost half-a-year like some dumb animal. This is my kill. I've earned this!" He left the spear sticking out of Gortrog. His body sat straight, leaning awkwardly against the spear like a scarecrow pole. Ollie reached down and lifted Gortrog's heavy sword, the green shard releasing an electric spasm wrapping around the wide blade.

The remaining warriors cheered in celebration as Myra covered Sariah's eyes. "That's it then. You've had your day. Can we please leave here before more of those beasts show up? We may not be this lucky next time."

"She's right," Jandar said, wincing in pain. "You can look at this like a victory, but the truth is, these were nothing more than patrol guards. When they come, they'll bring mercenaries known as elf-breakers. Like the ones that wiped out your village. We need to think ahead and determine our next move."

Jandar couldn't see much out of his good eye. He knew the deal. He would be so swollen that he couldn't see for a while, but he'd recover. For the time being, he'd be no good to anyone. He knew this spectacle would catch up to them. There was still the issue with Colvin the bounty hunter and his employers. He looked over at Colvin and nodded in appreciation yet wondered what favors he might owe him in return. *One thing at a time*, he thought.

"You need some help, old man?" Gymmal asked.

Jandar shook his head. "Unless you've got any bourbon, there's not much you can do, kid."

"I'm not sure I want this anymore. I'm tired of it all." Azoria, holding Myra's hand, reflected on all the trials that had brought them back together. She'd walked the forest alone, searching for her father's killer, the ravagers of her village, and the enslavers of her friends. The orcs had changed the course of their lives forever. There was no Averstone to go back to. But she found solace when she gazed over their unique team. Maybe it wasn't a team. Perhaps it was an unfortunate group of elf children bound by circumstances and, against all odds, achieved victory. But there were no medals to be awarded. This 'win' had broken something that could not be repaired.

Azoria had waited seasons for this opportunity. The preparation, the defeats, the training, and the journey. The relationship she'd forged with the blade. All to end here, witnessing the death of her arch-enemy. The one that had kept her awake at night. The monster who'd erased her father. And here they were, standing over the body of her lifeless nemesis. It didn't feel satisfying. None of it made sense to her. She looked out at the field, pushing the loose hair from out of her face. The dawn sun was breaking through the dark.

Azoria was weak. She leaned against her friends and the sword for support. Ollie walked to her. He unclenched his fist and dropped her father's bracelet in her palm. "You fought well. You, Azoria of the Dash Clan. You have the command of the warriors of Averstone."

Surprised, Azoria blushed. It was a rare sight for anyone to see. Then again, it was equally rare for Ollie to compliment anyone.

Azoria smiled and placed her hand over her heart in appreciation. "Thank you, General Ollie of the Stone Harpies."

"I'm hungry," Sariah said.

"I'm exhausted. I just want to sleep," said Myra with a yawn. "Where to now, Azoria? What do we do?"

Whether she knew it or not, Azoria was responsible for this team. Jandar noticed it too, and smiled. He thought about her as a lost child. He remembered the times he'd heard her laugh when she'd met Zuna. The brief moments when she'd forgotten how evil the world was, and just smiled like children did. The silly jokes she'd shared with Razzle or the smiles she'd given Gymmal when they'd found each other again. She was a child, growing into a deadly hunter. The insatiable hunger for revenge she possessed scared him the most. Many sides to one person, all just yearning to be in the arms of her friends. So young, yet so complex. Azoria was searching for love, for revenge. There she stood, broken yet stronger.

Azoria looked up at the stars, illuminating the depths of the vast universe that surrounded them. Like she did as a child, she counted the constellation's stars above. Unexpectedly, she counted one more star than usual. It was bright, and danced more radiant than the others. She smiled. "Meet you in the sky; just not tonight."

The surviving elves gathered around Azoria. They all looked at her, waiting for her response. There had been a time when she wouldn't have dared go past the creek. Now she lived amongst it, in the Crosslands.

*As the giant ellastrium ring shattered, the sorceress queen,
Vexa, opened her dark eyes.*

Book Two Coming Soon

Thank you for joining Azoria on her first of
what I hope to be many more adventures.
Kindly leave a review at wherever Azoria's
Blade is sold, including:
https://a.co/d/1Jb66GI

Instagram and Facebook @johndazebooks

To Illuminus!